KINGFISHER
An imprint of Kingfisher Publications Plc
New Penderel House, 283-288 High Holborn
London WC1V 7HZ
www.kingfisherpub.com

First published by Kingfisher 2007
2 4 6 8 10 9 7 5 3 1

A CIP catalogue record for this book
is available from the British Library.

ISBN: 978 07534 1166 7

Printed in China
1TR/1206/PROSP/SCHOY/70NEWSPRINT/C

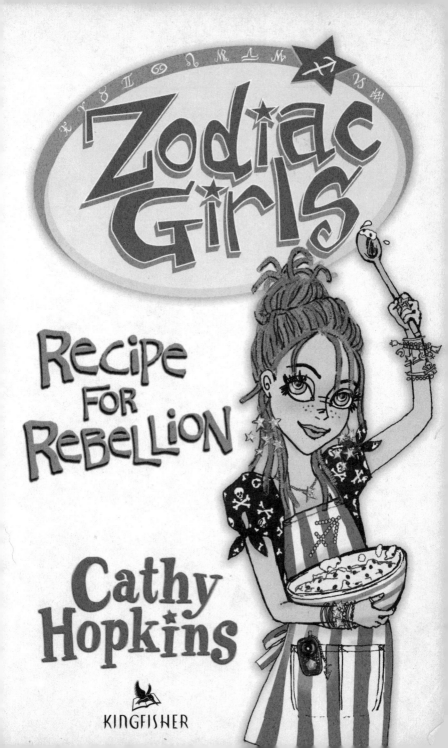

Zodiac Girls

Recipe for Rebellion

Cathy Hopkins

KINGFISHER

Chapter One

Bat poo

"Danu Harvey Jones. Can you read us the poem you've written about family?" asked Mr Beecham peering over his glasses at the front of the classroom. "And sit up straight, girl."

"It's Dee, not Danu," I said.

"I think not, Miss Harvey Jones. We call ourselves by our proper names at this school. We don't use nicknames and your given name is Danu. Now, stand up and read us your poem."

I stood up and took a deep breath.

"My aunt is full of bat poo,
My brother is a twit,
My parents have deserted me,
I don't know where I fit."

A few girls at the back of class tittered as Mr Beecham's mouth shrunk to look like a cat's bottom.

"That's enough Danu," he said. "Sit down. I don't think we need to hear any more of that. See me after class."

I sat down. I'd probably get detention again. I didn't care. At least there would be a few people around in there and it would be better than going back to the empty flat. Again.

Joele Morrison was next up reading her poem. I rolled my eyes. It was about a cute kitten playing on the grass and her ickle lickle baby brother rolling into a flower bed. Blah. Vomitous and a half. My poem had at least told the truth about my situation and what else was I supposed to write? About kittens and babies? Yeah right. A kitten would die of malnutrition where I was living now and as for an ickle lickle brother, there was just no space, in fact, there was only just enough space for me.

For the rest of the lesson as my fellow schoolmates droned on with their pathetic poems, I gazed out of the window and thought about my old life. What were my old friends doing at this moment as I sat here having to endure Death by Bad Poetry? I hated my life. I hated my new school. I hated everyone in it. My world was rotten. It wasn't always like this. I didn't always live in the hellhole that I do now. No. Once I had a life. A life I was very happy with thank you very much. I lived in a village down on the south coast with my dad who's an archaeologist. He's famous is some circles. My mum died when I was three so my dad had a lady from the

village come in and housekeep for us. Mrs Wilkins. She was lovely. Kind and jolly and the most brilliant cook. There was always the smell of something wonderful baking in the oven when I got home. I attended the local school and in fact I was able to walk there from our old house. It took ten minutes, through the back field, five minutes along the coast road and there I was. I had loads of mates. Bernie, Fran, Annie and Jane. I had a dog, Snowy (he was jet black). I had a cat, Blackie (he was pure white) and I used to be able to ride our neighbour's horse. They let me name him so I called him Spot (he was a chestnut). There were birds and squirrels in our garden. I had a huge bedroom with a bay window looking out over rolling fields and woods. I was happy.

One day, Dad was waiting for me when I came home from school. I could tell the moment I set eyes on him that something was wrong. At first I thought someone had died or something had happened to Snowy or Blackie. But no. Nothing like that. Dad had been offered a year's contract working on some ancient site in South America digging up old bones and stuff. Chance of a lifetime. The one he'd been waiting for. Etc etc. Blah de blah de blah. And that was the end of life as I knew it.

Why couldn't he go and leave me with Mrs Wilkins as usually happened when there was a dig?

I asked. But he wouldn't hear of it. Other digs had been for a weekend, a fortnight at the longest. This was the big one and would take him away for a whole year. I begged to be able to stay at the house but he'd already arranged for it to be rented out for the year. Nothing I could say or do could persuade him to let me stay. I tried to fix it so I could live with one of my mates but no-one had room. I'd be "just fine," said Dad. He'd arranged for me to attend a boarding school near where his sister lived. He'd be back to see me in the holidays and my aunt would keep an eye on me in the meantime. I was a grown up girl. I'd soon adjust. That was the time I realized that he cared more about a load of old dead bones than he did about me, his living daughter.

"Danu, *Danu*," said a stern voice in my ear. It was old Beecham again. What did he want now?

"Yes, sir."

"Have you been listening to anything that is going on in this lesson?"

"Yes, sir. Kittens. Ickle babies."

Mr Beecham sighed then went back to the front of the room. "Class dismissed," he said.

I got up to go with the others.

"Not you, Harvey Jones. I want a word."

I slumped back down into my chair. I was very popular with the teachers at this school. They were always keeping me back for "a word".

Mr Beecham waited as the rest of the class filed out. A few of the girls turned and stared at me then whispered to each other. I stuck my tongue out at them.

When the others had gone, Mr Beecham came and sat at the desk opposite and looked at me with concern.

"So Danu. How are you settling in?"

I shrugged. "Okay."

He sighed again. "And how's life at home?"

"Not at home..."

"Ah yes, I meant your home now. I believe you're living with your aunt?"

I shrugged again. "Yeah."

"And are things all right there?"

"Yeah." I wasn't going to tell him the truth. There was no point. Nobody could do anything to get me out of there.

Mr Beecham coughed. "Well Danu... I'm afraid we're going to have to do something, aren't we? About your attitude."

I shifted my feet and looked out of the window.

"Have you got any suggestions?" Mr Beecham persisted. "And please look at me when I'm talking to you."

I turned back to him. "Whatever."

"Whatever is not an answer. I have your records

from your past school, Danu, so you don't fool me. You were a straight-A pupil and now your highest mark is D. What are you going to do about it?"

"Work harder," I muttered. I had no intention of working harder. My plan was to get expelled and then with a bit of luck, I could go back to my old school. Even if it meant living in the dog kennel with Snowy, I wouldn't mind.

Mr Beecham stood up. "I hope so Danu. I hope so. We're here to help you know, not hinder, so I'd appreciate a bit of an effort on your part. And... I also need to talk to you about... well about your hair..."

"What about it?" I asked. It had taken me months to get it into decent dreadlocks. As my hair is fine and reddish blonde, it had taken weeks and weeks of twirling and twirling before the coils stayed but at last they were starting to look the business. I'd even wound some green and pink wool through some of them. My dreadlocks were part of my plan. I had to look the part of a rebel as well as act it.

"Well... don't you ever comb it?"

"No way."

"But that can't be hygienic."

I shrugged. "Is there a rule that says I can't wear my hair like this?"

"Not exactly."

"So what's the problem?"

"It makes you look, well, how can I put this… rather unkempt."

"Do you tell other girls how to wear their hair?"

"No. I don't make a habit of it."

"Right then. Can I go now?"

Mr Beecham sighed. "I suppose so."

I made my way out of the school and through the playground to the bus stop. Girls were still hanging about, chatting, having a laugh. I kept my head down. I wished I had a mate here. I wished I had someone's house I could go to and hang out in, gossiping about the day, about fellow pupils. But no, the only place I had to go back to was the prison of a flat where I lived with my aunt, the warden.

She lives in a small flat on the fifteenth floor of a tall block in a new development area. No grass, no trees, no animals and no outside access except for a tiny balcony with one dead pot plant on it. Aunt Esme earns good dosh at her job but she chooses to live in this no man's land because it's an easy commute to her work. Okay for her as she's never home. I felt like I was suffocating there. There's nothing to do. Nowhere to go as it's not safe after dark because of its proximity to a rough estate. I was going to end up like that poor geranium on the balcony. Dead.

I caught the bus and sat looking out at the gloomy winter's night. The clocks had gone back last week so it was dark early. On the streets, people were huddled into their coats rushing to get home out of the cold. I got off in the square where Aunt Esme lives and sloped over to her block. Up the steps, into the door, into the lift that smelt damp, of boiled cabbage, and up to her floor. It was like being in some sci fi film about the future where all traces of natural life had been destroyed and all that was left was concrete.

I let myself into the flat, turned on the lights and went into the sitting room to turn on the TV. I always did that the minute I got back as the sounds of people on the telly made me feel as if I wasn't totally alone. I slumped down to watch. No point in going to the fridge. Aunt Esme didn't buy proper food, only posh assorted lettuce in polythene bags. And sometimes there was a lemon in there for her gin and tonic drink. She never cooked at home as she ate out most evenings with her job or grabbed something at the office where she usually worked late.

At six o'clock precisely there was a knock at the door. It was Rosa bringing my supper. She works as Aunt Esme's cleaner and when I moved in, she was hired to bring me my supper every evening as well. She's Polish, about twenty, and hardly speaks any

English.

She came into the hall and pointed towards the kitchen.

"Shall put in microwiv?" she asked.

"No, I'll take it," I replied. "Thank you."

She handed me the dish then left.

She wasn't a bad cook actually, although her repertoire was somewhat limited. Some sort of goulashy thing with carrots and beans every night. *Still better than soggy lettuce*, I thought as I heated it up and took it back to eat while I watched TV.

I'd heated it up too much and the first forkful burnt the inside of my mouth. I felt tears prick the back of my eyes.

"Bat poo," I said to the empty room.

I had never felt so alone in all of my life.

Chapter Two

Aunt Esme

"Danu, come and clear up this mess this instant," called Aunt Esme from the sitting room the following morning.

I was in my bedroom emailing my old mates. I switched off the computer and went to face the firing squad. What did she want now?

In the living room, Aunt Esme was dressed in her usual black business suit, white shirt, dark hair tied back in a neat bun and she was busy dusting the shelves. She was mental. She cleaned up after Rosa had been *and* before she came.

"What mess?" I asked. The room looked fine to me. It always did. Okay, the carpet was a bit faded but there wasn't anything to mess up. One L-shaped cream Italian sofa still with its polythene wrapping on (in case anything got spilled on it). A faded cream carpet (Aunt Esme said she'd get round to replacing it one day but at the moment was too busy, busy, busy). White walls with no pictures. A set of bookshelves with only a Yellow Pages directory and an A – Z on it. A glass coffee table. One square glass vase in an empty fireplace. No flowers in it. I hated the place. She hadn't even got round to putting any curtains or blinds up at the windows. It was the coldest room I'd ever set eyes on, not the kind of place you could curl up and be cosy in, but then Aunt Esme never did that. All she did was work, work, work. She's a lawyer in the city and lives and breathes her job.

Aunt Esme pointed at the supper dishes which were still on the coffee table from last night.

"I've told you before about clearing up after yourself. It's really not too much to ask is it? You know I don't have time when I get back from work," she glanced at her watch, "and I certainly don't have time now as I have to go into the office."

"And a good morning to you too," I said.

"No need to be sarcastic," said Aunt Esme.

"I was going to do the dishes. Honest. Give me a break."

Aunt Esme made an effort to force a smile but it came out more like a grimace. "So what are you going to do with yourself today?"

"Nothing. There's nothing to do."

"Homework?"

"Done it." I hadn't but she didn't need to know that.

"Then do you want to go and get a couple of DVDs from the corner shop?"

"*Again*? I think I've seen everything they have there. I'd hoped maybe we could do something. Go somewhere."

"Danu, I can't. Really. I have a major case on at the moment and it's taking every minute I've got."

I slumped down on the sofa.

"Feet, feet," said Aunt Esme swatting my legs off her sofa.

"I've got clean socks on," I objected. "And the sofa's covered."

"I don't care. We don't put our feet on the furniture in this house."

"Don't do this, don't do that. It's like living in a prison there are so many rules."

Aunt Esme sighed. "My house, my rules. You knew that when you came here."

"It's not a house. It's a flat."

"Oh don't be difficult, Danu. You know what I meant." She glanced at her watch again. "Have you had breakfast?"

"Like you care."

Aunt Esme sighed. "Actually I do care. Have you had something?"

"Yes. I had dried yak's buttock and a slice of lemon. It was all that was in the fridge."

"Very funny. Rosa will be in this evening as usual with your supper but what about lunch? I'll leave you some money and you can get yourself something."

"Whatever."

Aunt Esme put on her jacket and found her bag. "Right then. See you later."

I flicked on the TV. "Later."

Aunt Esme hovered for a minute. "Look I know I've been busy lately and I'm sorry. Haven't you made any new friends at the school you can see?"

"They all hate me."

"I'm sure they don't."

"Do."

Aunt Esme sighed again and rooted round in her bag for her purse. "Look I can't get into this now. Here's twenty pounds, get yourself some lunch. In fact, make it thirty. Take ten for some pocket money. And oh, can you get a couple of lemons while you're out."

"Whatever…" *Pocket money. Pfff,* I thought. *What was I going to spend that on round here?*

"And *stop* saying 'whatever'. It's driving me mad." She picked up her bag and for a moment hovered at the door. She looked awkward. "Er… um… Danu… I… I also wanted to mention something. Um. Week after next I have to go to New York…"

"New York! For how long?"

"Oh not long. Only a week."

"But… the week after next is not just any old week. It's half term. What about me?"

Now Aunt Esme did look uncomfortable. "Half term. Oh god I didn't realize. Listen. Don't worry. I've asked Rosa if she can stay while I'm away and she's agreed so you won't be on your own."

I crossed my arms over my stomach. "Like anyone cares."

A look of exasperation flashed across Aunt Esme's face. "What else can I do Danu? It's part of my job. I've always had to travel from time to time and I told your father that before you came here."

"He doesn't care either," I said. "Go to New York. I don't care at all. In fact I hate you. And Dad. I hate everyone."

"We'll talk about it later," said Aunt Esme and she was out the door in a flash, leaving me alone once again. *Huh,* I thought, *go to New York. It's not as if you're here and we spend any time together when you're in England. I don't care. I won't care.* I gazed at the telly. *Saturday morning TV. My new friend,* I thought as I flicked channels. *My only friend.* I never used to watch telly down in Dorset at the weekend. I had too many things to do. Places to go. Jaunts out with Bernie, Jane, Annie and Fran. A ride through the village on Spot. A walk over the fields with Snowy. I hoped that

Snowy and Blackie were all right with their new owners. The family that had taken over our old house had children and they loved pets so it was decided that ours should stay so that they didn't get disrupted. Huh. Not that I begrudged them being allowed to stay as I wanted them to be happy but it seemed that even the animals' feelings were taken into consideration more than mine.

I watched TV for an hour or so, did a bit of homework. Emailed my mates again. Then sat and stared at a wall. I remembered seeing a film once where the woman in it talked to the wall in her kitchen. *Shirley Valentine*, that's what it was called. I thought she was mad at the time but now, I could totally relate.

"Okay wall, what shall I do today?"

It didn't reply. I didn't think it would. That really would be bonkers. I got up to look out of the window. Another grey November day. Still not raining at least. I never used to mind the coming of winter in the country as each new season brought new colours and new scents. Back at home, the leaves would be just coming down off the trees covering the fields in carpets of glorious reds, oranges and yellows. The air would be crisp and cold and would smell of burning leaves. Here, there were only grey paving stones. No colour at all. And the only smell was from rotten food in the rubbish bins round the back of the flats.

Maybe I'll go and have a wander down to the corner shop, I thought as I stared out. *Buy some baked beans or something madly exciting like that.*

I grabbed my coat and scarf and made my way out of the block, through the square and over to the corner shop run by Mr Patel where I bought a loaf of bread and pot noodles then looked at the DVDs at the back of the store in the hope that he had something new. But no. I'd seen them all.

As I was crossing back over the square again, I noticed a small crowd had gathered near the abstract round sculpture in the middle. *What were they watching?* I wondered. Nothing ever happened round here. Surely they couldn't be admiring the sculpture as it was an enormous round granite ball. Not worth looking at really.

I joined the group and stood on tiptoe to try and see over their shoulders. Mrs Patel, the corner shop owner's wife saw me and moved to her left so that I could see better. She was there with her daughter, Sushila, who glanced at me and smiled in acknowledgement. I knew her vaguely as she went to the same school and often caught the same bus as me. But we'd never spoken because she always seemed to be surrounded by her friends.

In the middle of the crowd was a street performer balancing on a unicycle. He (or at least I thought he was a he. He had such delicate features that he could have been a she) looked like he was in his early twenties and was dressed in an electric blue bodysuit with a silver lightning streak painted across his face. *Definitely a he,* I decided as I took in the slim flat chested body and long legs. He was moving in clockwise circles and juggling balls. He looked wonderful, a blast of colour against the grey sky and buildings. I stood and watched for a while then when it was over, he started to hand out leaflets. *Some business promotion,* I reckoned and began to walk away.

"Hey, you, gloomy girl," called the juggler.

I turned back to see the man approaching me. *What a cheek,* I thought, *calling me gloomy. What did he know?*

"Surprise," he said. With a flourish, he handed me a leaflet.

I glanced at it. It seemed to be advertising a café of some kind.

"Yeah right," I said. "Big surprise. What are you selling exactly?"

"Not selling. Just letting you know."

"Know what?"

"About Europa."

"Which is?"

"A Greek deli," he grinned. "Best in the area."

"A deli? Round here? Now that is a surprise. You're kidding."

"No I'm not. Expect the unexpected. You should go. Cheer you up. It's good."

I hate people who tell me to cheer up so I gave him a withering look but he grinned back at me. I glanced down at the leaflet again. It was covered in planets and stars and on the back was printed a menu. *Maybe I should go,* I thought. The dishes listed looked a lot more appetising than the pot noodle I had in my carrier bag.

"Okay then, where is it?" I asked. "I've never seen a deli, in fact, I've hardly seen any shops."

The juggler looked at me and sighed then said very slowly as if I was stupid, "So... travel. Get... a... bus..."

"What bus?"

The man pointed towards the bus stop. "Number 73. Takes you right there."

The 73 is my school bus. I'd never noticed a village on the way so maybe it was in the other direction.

Mrs Patel nodded her head. "He's right. The 73 takes you right into Osbury. Very popular place. Nice village."

Popular place. Nice village. How come Aunt Esme

had never told me about this place? Then again, she never went anywhere locally. Only ever took her train into town returning again late at night. She'd probably never been to Osbury.

"I'm going in with Sushila on the next bus," said Mrs Patel. "And I know that café and the owner. You want to come with us?"

I considered my options. The empty flat, morning TV and pot noodles. More history homework. Or a trip to discover a village where there was a deli selling tantalising sounding meals. And Aunt Esme had said, get yourself some lunch. There might even be some interesting shops nearby to mooch around in and kill some time.

"Whatever," I shrugged and followed Mrs Patel to the bus stop.

"Whatever," said the juggler mimicking my voice and getting off his unicycle to wearily slope after me like he was my shadow. My shadow with rounded shoulders. Mrs Patel laughed but I wanted to sock him. I didn't look or sound *that* bad and I certainly didn't walk with such round shoulders. As we stood waiting for the bus, he gave us a wave then went off to collect his things from the middle of the square. When the bus arrived, my last glimpse of him was on his cycle, a bright blue umbrella in one hand, riding in circles around the sculpture.

Chapter Three

Joe

The bus wove its way through street after boring street. New houses, high-rise blocks of flats similar to Aunt Esme's, paved squares, past our school, another housing development. I couldn't imagine a village in amongst all this. It was a concrete jungle. Grey and heartless. Then suddenly, there was a field. And another one. The view was opening up. Trees! Space. Colour. Leaves in soft yellows, vivid oranges, deep reds. Fields of grass still green from the summer sun. Even the clouds seemed to be giving way to a clear blue winter sky. I began to feel like I could breathe again.

"Not far now," said Mrs Patel from the seat in front of me.

"I never imagined that we were so near to the country."

Sushila looked at me as if I was mad so I went back to gazing out of the window. Past an old lodge called Chiron House, then a huge wrought iron gate that had the name Avebury on it. *Oh. So that's where it is*, I thought. That was the school I was meant to have gone to. A private boarding school. Dad had filled in all the applications, put them somewhere safe then forgotten to send them off. Typical. My dad might be considered in some circles to be one of the brains of Britain but he was hopeless when it came to organising anything. Dizzy when it came to the domestic. By the time he realized that he'd neglected to send the application off, all the places at Avebury had been taken. Not that I wanted to go there at the time but it might have been better than where I ended up. At least at Avebury all the pupils were boarders and I'd have had company.

There was an almighty last minute panic when Dad had realized his mistake, like, what are we going to do with Danu? Dad's flights had been booked. Everything was arranged. For him. Frantic phone calls were made. He even considered sending me to Brighton to be near my brother Luke who's at university there but that was soon vetoed as Luke lives in student lodgings and Dad feared that I'd be led into evil studenty ways and turn into a drug addict or a psychopath. Aunt Esme was our last option and she wasn't too keen on the idea of having me live with her full time. That wasn't part of her plan. If I'd gone to Avebury, I'd only have had to stay with her at

Christmas, Easter and in the summer. Dad did his grovelling act to talk her into it, saying that she was going to have had me in the holidays anyway. In the end, she gave in. She even found me a place in the local school. If it had been left to Dad, I might have ended up living with Aunt Esme and attending school a million miles away.

"Our stop," said Mrs Patel as the bus made a turn then drove into a street that was lined on both sides with shops and cafés. At one end, I could see an old church with a steeple, church hall and a green in front. At the other end of the street was a bus shelter, a phone box and post box.

"Brilliant," I said, rising to get off with the Patels when the bus stopped. A place to explore. I couldn't wait.

"I'm getting the bus back at four," said Mrs Patel. "You can come back with me if you like or later with Sushila."

Sushila didn't say anything. She saw a bunch of her mates hanging out by the shelter and took off with a brief, "later," to her mum.

"Thank you, Mrs Patel," I said. "I'd like that." I can be polite if I want to be and I even smiled which is something I hadn't done for weeks.

Mrs Patel took off towards a florist's so I stood at the bus stop and tried to decide where to go first. I felt like a kid at Christmas who thought she'd got no presents, then discovers a Santa's grotto full of them. Osbury looked to be a quaint village, reminiscent of home. As I strolled along to the left, I spotted Europa, the deli. *I won't go there yet*, I thought. *I'll save it for later*. Next to the deli was a beauty salon called Pentangle. Opposite was an optician's, a chemist's, a mini supermarket. *Plenty to look at*, I thought as I passed a tanning salon, a couple of clothes shops, an interior design shop, a fish-and-chip shop and a party and magic shop with what looked like a cyber café at the back. A magic shop? I peered in through the window. To my amazement, I could see the juggler who'd been in the square earlier! He was serving behind the counter. He looked up and gave me a wave. *How did he get back here so fast?* I wondered. He wasn't on the bus with us. He beckoned me to go in.

I didn't hesitate as his shop window looked interesting with a good number of items that would come in handy for the next stage of my plan to get kicked out of school. I decided to go in and have a closer look.

"Hi gloomy girl," said the juggler as soon as I walked in.

"My name is Danu, actually," I said as I glanced around. "*Not* gloomy girl. But you can call me Dee."

The shop interior was futuristic in style with a

number of top-of-the-range computers in the back area where a couple of customers appeared to be surfing the internet. The front of the shop was painted electric blue with silver flashes across the ceiling, not unlike the juggler's costume and face paint.

"Danu. How fabulous. Oh you mustn't shorten it to Dee. It's the name of a goddess."

"Wow!" I said with genuine amazement. "You're the first person I've ever met who knows that apart from my parents."

"Oh I think you'll find a lot of people here in Osbury are up on their gods and goddesses. My name is Uri," said the juggler as he leaned over the counter to shake my hand. I took his hand to shake it back and a loud buzzer went off giving me an electric shock. It didn't hurt but I wasn't expecting it and almost leapt out of my skin.

"Perfect," I said. "Can I buy one of those?"

Uri grinned. "You can indeed. Planning to surprise someone?"

"A few someones actually. What else have you got?"

"What haven't we got?" asked Uri, then proceeded to show me half the contents of his shop: itching powder, blood capsules, fake dog poop, soap that makes your face dirty, a remote control fart machine, an exploding pen... There were all sorts of wonderful practical jokes and tricks and I left half an hour later with a carrier bag full of purchases to try out at school next week.

After the magic shop, I went into a couple of clothes shops and tried on a few T-shirts and tops. I had a browse in a bookshop and began to enjoy myself for the first time in weeks. It certainly beat how I'd spent the last few weekends, on my own having one-sided conversations with walls.

After mooching about for a while, I began to feel hungry. Someone walked past me with a bag of chips and the alluring smell of salt and vinegar made me realize that it was time for lunch. I looked around for a fish-and-chip shop and soon spied a likely place across the road. The door was painted with a picture of a bearded man with a trident in one hand and a fish in the other. The shop was called Poseidon. *That must be it*, I thought as I crossed the road. The door chinked open and inside I could see a man with a white beard not unlike the man in the painting on the door. He was serving a customer. When he'd finished, he turned to me and did a double take.

"Oh. It's you," he said as if he was unhappy to see me.

I looked around. I didn't know him so why had he said, "oh it's you," like we'd met before and he didn't want to see me.

"Um, fish and chips, please."

The man pulled a silver cover down over his chips. "Sorry. We're closed," he said. "Try the deli."

"But…." I'd seen that there were loads of fish and chips left. Why was he turning me away? "But there are loads here."

"Lunch break," he said. "Closed."

I felt my mouth watering. "Please, can't you just serve me then close for lunch? I'm starving."

The man shook his head. "Closed. Try the deli." He came out from behind the counter and went to the door where he pulled down a blind. "Off you go."

Mean man, I thought as I went back out into the street. I felt hurt by his rejection. It was so totally what I didn't need at this stage in my life.

Maybe this village isn't so nice after all, I thought as I bit back sudden tears.

I made my way over to the deli and peered in the window. It looked cosy in there. *Should I risk being rejected again?* I asked myself. *Maybe the people in there are mean as well.* My tummy rumbling gave me my answer. *I'd better get in fast,* I thought, *in case they want to close for lunch as well.* I opened the door to see that there were about eight wooden tables, most of which were occupied with customers tucking into large steaming plates of food. The smell of garlic and onions filled the air and my mouth started watering again. I felt as if I hadn't had a proper meal in ages.

At the back of the deli was a big jolly-looking man with a round belly who was slicing tomatoes. He was wearing a navy apron printed with the planets and stars – the same design that was on his leaflet. When he saw me, his rosy face broke into a huge grin.

"Hey. *There* you are," he said coming towards me with his arms open in a welcoming gesture. For a moment, I thought he was going to hug me so I took a step back and turned around to make sure he wasn't looking at someone else. But no, it was definitely me. *What was it with this village?* I wondered. *Everyone seems to think they know me. At least this guy looks friendly unlike his fishy neighbour.*

"Um. Yes. Here I am. You are open for lunch, aren't you?"

"What does it look like?" smiled the man as he ushered me to a table in the corner then thrust a menu into my hand. "You look hungry. What would you like?"

I glanced over the menu. It all sounded wonderful. Some Greek dishes, some Italian.

"I'm Joe," said the chubby man. "Joe Joeve. Now, let me get you something to drink while you choose."

I watched him go back to the counter, smiling and beaming at everyone. Clearly he was like this with all his customers, greeting everyone like they were a long-lost friend. I wasn't going to object. I could do with a long lost friend at the moment.

Two minutes later, he was back with a big mug of what looked like hot cocoa. "Made with real chocolate," he said as he placed it in front of me. "And melted marshmallows. So what will it be?"

"Um, today's special please."

"One special with chorizo and beans coming up," he said and with another big smile, he was off again.

As I sat waiting for lunch, I glanced at a small bookshelf to my left. It was full of books. Travel books I noticed. To the right of my table was a notice board. There was a mishmash of leaflets announcing local events pinned up there. Fêtes, book fairs, jam sales, birthday cake makers, people offering to walk your dog, babysitters, bikes for sale, a man who could fix lawn mowers.

I felt a wave of sadness come over me. This village and particularly the cafe, reminded me of all that I'd left behind. A sense of community. Familiarity. Belonging. I'd taken it all for granted at the time. Back home, I'd walk through our village and everyone would either stop to stroke Snowy or enquire after my dad. I knew all the shopkeepers and their families. I'd known them all my life. And there was always something going on. A choir at Christmas. Cake sales at Easter. Fêtes in summer. Trick or treat on

Halloween. Bonfire and fireworks on Guy Fawkes. Living at Aunt Esme's felt like living in a wasteland. People didn't know or talk to their neighbours. People were careful not to make eye contact. I knew no-one apart from the Patels and that was only because I shopped at their corner shop.

I got out my phone and scrolled through for Dad's number. He'd said that I could call him any time, anywhere. I pressed his number and waited. As usual, his phone was on voice mail. Dad hadn't quite joined this century regarding mobiles. He got the concept that it was a phone that you could take anywhere but hadn't quite grasped the fact that you had to keep them turned *on* and the battery topped up. I was forever having to recharge his for him when he was home. Without me there to remind him, he'd probably let it go flat.

I decided to leave a message in the hope that he'd remember to pick up his voice messages or top up his battery sometime. Somehow I doubted it though. He could decipher ancient alphabets and translate almost extinct languages but the chances of him picking up a message in this century from a live person were next to none.

"Hi Dad," I said. "I want to beg you one last time, please, please, please can I go home and back to my old school. It's not working here. I hate it. I've never been so miserable. I know I'm only almost thirteen, and you're mainly interested in things that are at least two thousand but please listen. Everyone hates me. I don't belong…" Suddenly I jumped. Joe was standing to the side of me and it seemed as if he might have heard so I clicked the phone off. He was looking at me with the saddest expression. "Oh dear," he said with a shake of his head. "Oh dear oh dear oh dear."

I felt myself start to blush. Was he mocking me? I wasn't sure. I gave him my best "I don't care" look and tried to pretend that I hadn't been begging my dad to let me go home a minute earlier.

"Is that my lunch?" I asked in my best grown-up voice.

Joe nodded. He sat down opposite and put a steaming bowl of casserole in front of me. It smelt wonderful, of sausages and herbs.

"I'm so sorry to hear that you've been miserable," he said. "Is best when everyone is happy. And *I* don't hate you. Not everybody hates you. Perhaps…"

"That was a private phone call," I said again in my grown-up voice.

Joe got up. "Of course. None of my business. So eat. Enjoy. Tomorrow may be better."

I kept my head down and began eating. It was the most delicious food I'd had in ages. Even better than

Mrs Wilkins used to cook and she was good. Joe was still standing there watching me.

I glanced up at him. "What?"

"I meant it when I said that tomorrow may be better. Life, the universe, your experience of it," said Joe. "Everything changes. Nothing lasts forever. Things will get better."

"Whatever," I said.

"Whatever," he smiled back.

With that, he went over to his counter then came back with what looked like another leaflet for the shop as it was covered in the same planets and stars.

"Got one," I said through a mouthful of food.

"No?" said Joe looking down. "When?"

"Um, juggler this morning in the square where I live."

"You mean Uri from the party shop. No. That leaflet was for my café to bring you here. No, this is different. Look again." He pushed the leaflet back in front of me.

This time I had a proper look. It was for a web site. Something to do with astrology.

"Check it out," said Joe. "It will be good for you. Make you happier."

"Mmff," I said as I finished my lunch. I wanted to be left alone. I didn't want anyone sitting too close in case I cracked in front of them and they saw that I wasn't hard, without a care in the world. I wasn't as grown-up as I acted. Inside I was lost and sad and lonely. "I will, I will." I was quite interested in astrology. Back home Fran, Annie, Jane, Bernie and I used to read our horoscopes regularly and it wouldn't do any harm to check out what the stars had in store for me here in my new life.

"You make sure you do," said Joe then he began to sing. "Nobody loves me. Everybody hates me. I think I'll go and eat worms. Big ones, fat ones, short ones, thin ones, see how the little one squirms."

I almost laughed.

Chapter Four
Site for sore eyes

As soon as I got back to the flat in the early evening, I went into my routine.

Put on the lights. "Let there be light. Ta daah."

Put on the TV. "Let there be sound. Ta daah."

Checked the answering machine. "Let there be messages for me from friends in the great big world."

There was one: "Hi Danu. Esme here. Look sorry about this morning. Hope you haven't been sitting in all on your own. Be back as soon as I can. Oh got to go, other line's going…"

I felt bad I'd given her such a hard time earlier especially as I'd had such a good day. She's not so bad really and she had taken me in at the last moment. It can't have been easy having a teenage girl move into your personal space.

Checked my emails: Inbox: (4)

One from Fran:

Watcha wombat. Hope you're hanging well. Notalot to report. School muchos dulloss. New

teacher for anglaisie who is mega allergic and keeps sneezing. Don't think she's going to last long. Asnuh, asnuh, achooo. Miss you missmostmuch.

One from Bernie:

Hi Dee hi, hi dee hoh. Um. Don't know what to write today. Got a spot on my chin. Put toothpaste on it. Stings a bit. Um. That's all.

One from Jane:

Come home now. All is forgiven and we miss you. I so wish we could find somewhere for you to stay. If I killed my brother, you could have his bed but he refuses to drink the poison.

One from Annie:

Hey Dee. What's happening in your neck of the woods? Hope you've settled in some more as you sounded majorly down last week and I hate to think of you being mis and lonely. Stay in touch. And hopefully we can come visit or you can come here. Been keeping an eye on Spot and he looks fine. Rosie Peters from Year Eleven has been riding him so he's okay and getting exercise. And I dropped in to see Snowy and Blackie and they're both A-OK. I also saw Mrs Wilkins in the village yesterday and she said to pass on her best love. Wish you were still here. It's weird without you. Loads of love.

They've been good mates and made a real effort to stay in touch because they all knew that one of my biggest fears was that we'd drift apart because of distance. I don't believe the saying that goes "absence makes the heart grow fonder". I think absence makes the heart forget. Like Dad does about me when he goes off on one of his digs.

I was about to close down the computer when I remembered what Joe had said about trying his website. He was a jolly old soul, if a bit mad but then I liked mad people usually, they made life more interesting. I found my jacket and rooted around in the pocket for the leaflet then took it back to my desk. I logged onto the web and typed in the address.

It took a moment for the site to download and slowly the screen began to fill with the image of a night sky full of stars and planets. Soft spacey music began to play.

As I waited, I decided that I'd find my horoscope, (Sagittarius) and maybe the other girls (Fran/Taurus, Bernie/Cancer, Annie/Virgo, Jane/Capricorn) and send them theirs as a surprise. Fran would like that as she's really into astrology.

I looked for the list of the twelve signs that are usually on astrology websites but there was only a form to fill in. *Ah well, why not?* I thought. I'd had a good day after having met Uri. Why not see where this led as well. I began to type in my details.

Name: Danu Norwan Harvey Jones.

39

My dad chose my names. Danu after a West European goddess. It means great mother. Norwan is a Northern American goddess and the name means dancing porcupine. Annie, Jane, Fran and Bernie are the only other people in the whole world who know the origin and meaning of my names and they were sworn to secrecy in a ceremony performed when we were nine years old. We each put our biggest secrets on a piece of paper in a Chinese box and buried it in a secret place in the woods near our old house. That was the day that it was decided that from thence on, I should be called Dee but no-one remembers to call me that apart from them. Not even Dad or Luke and I've told them a million times.

Birth date and place. December 18th, Dorset, England.

Time: 7.45pm. Luckily I knew my time of birth as my dad told me that he thought I was very considerate being born when I was. I was a home delivery and there was a programme he wanted to watch about Egyptian mummies on the telly at eight o'clock and he was worried that he was going to miss it because Mum was still in labour. Then out I popped, just in time for him to make Mum, himself and the midwife a cup of tea and settle down to watch his programme (even then he was more concerned with old bones than new).

As soon as I'd completed the form on the screen, it swirled away as if evaporating. Then suddenly the computer screen began to flash on and off like a strobe light at a disco. I thought something was wrong and it was going to blow up or crash but the screen soon cleared and up came the words CONGRATULATIONS in red and gold accompanied by a drum roll crescendo and a blast of trumpets.

The words YOU ARE THIS MONTH'S ZODIAC GIRL!!!!!!! flashed across the screen. I chuckled to myself. *Hey Joe, do you think we're all stupid out here?* I thought. This month's Zodiac Girl? Yeah right. Me and a million others. D'er. I'm Sagittarius. Anyone born from November 23rd to December 21st is this month's Zodiac Girl. No big deal. Someone must have persuaded Joe to use astrology as a promotion for his business. Maybe one day, I'd pop into the deli and tell him that the site only stated the obvious. *Shame that was all there was*, I thought, as I switched off the computer and went to do some homework before Rosa arrived with my supper.

Just as I was settling down to watch telly, I heard a knock at the door.

"Won't be a mo, Rosa," I called out thinking that she was early with my supper tonight.

I went to open the door and found Sushila standing

there. She thrust a padded envelope at me.

"You left your phone in the café in Osbury," she said. "Joe asked me to give it back to you."

"Oh! I never even realized," I said as I took the package although I could have sworn that I had it with me when I left the deli. "Er… thanks."

I was about to close the door but she was still standing there.

"Sorry. Was there something else?" I asked.

"Not very friendly are you?" she asked.

I shrugged. I'd learnt that it was best to stay neutral in my new life. No expectations, no disappointments. I was a new girl in a school where all the friendships had already been established. I'd learnt to keep my head down, keep myself to myself. That way, I wasn't let down.

Sushila was still standing there. "So… gonna invite me in?"

"In? Er… yeah. If you like."

"Great," said Sushila stepping inside. "I've always wanted to look in one of these flats."

I led her through to the sitting room where she took in the sparse decor.

"Wow," she said. "You only just moved here?"

"I've only been here a short while," I explained. "It's my Aunt Esme's place. She's lived here for a few years but she uses it like a hotel."

"A few years? Really? You wouldn't think so. It feels like it's brand new. Like it's picture perfect but unlived in."

"Exactly my sentiments," I said as Sushila nosed around a bit more and looked at the non view out of the window.

I began to feel like an estate agent showing a prospective buyer around as I led her through the rest of the flat.

"And this Modom, is our small but efficient kitchen. As you'll see all mod cons in order to cut down cooking to a minimum. Microwave, kettle, fridge."

Sushila didn't comment just nodded and poked her nose into a couple of cupboards.

"Where's the food?" she asked when she saw that most of them were empty.

"Aunt Esme hardly ever eats at home," I explained and led her out of the kitchen and towards the bathroom.

"Next is the bathroom, size of a cupboard I know but then it probably was a cupboard."

"Yeah, not bad," said Sushila as she took a quick peek, then I took her into Aunt Esme's room which, like the rest of the flat, was painted white and had the minimum of furniture. I opened her closets to reveal rows of colour co-ordinated clothes. Not that there were many colours to co-ordinate: black, grey, navy, beige. I couldn't resist opening her drawers too.

"Woah!" said Sushila when she saw the rows of neatly folded knickers. "Looks like she *irons* her underwear."

"She irons everything. That is when she's not dusting. I think she's one of those obsessive compulsive people. A major control freak."

Sushila went back into the corridor so I followed after her.

"My room," I said when she stuck her head in the last door.

"I gathered that," she said. "It's the only room that looks lived in. Although you haven't unpacked all your stuff."

I stepped over the boxes she was looking at. I hadn't unpacked everything partly because there was nowhere to put things and partly because I was hoping that I wouldn't be staying too long.

"My room back home was four times the size," I said.

"So what are you doing here?"

I shrugged. "I stare at walls a lot. Watch telly…"

"No. I mean, what are you doing here?" She gestured the flat.

"Existing. Breathing. Same as everyone else."

Sushila sighed. "I *meant*, where's your mum and dad?"

I led her back into the sitting room and so that she couldn't see my face, I explained on the way. "My mum died when I was three and my dad's gone off on a job somewhere in the mountains of Peru."

"What does he do?" asked Sushila.

"Digs old bones up."

Sushila laughed. "Sounds like our dog. He does that. Bet he never thought of it as a job!"

I laughed with her. "Dad writes about them and puts them in museums."

"Cool."

"Is for him."

"Ah. You don't want to be here?"

I shook my head. "Nope."

"I'm sorry your mum died."

"So am I."

"Got any brothers or sisters anywhere?"

I nodded and almost laughed. She reminded me of me. Always asking questions, no matter how awkward. "Luke. He's at university in Brighton."

Sushila glanced at her watch. "Oops, got to go. It's my birthday today and Mum's cooking something special. You eaten?"

I shook my head. "I have my supper delivered."

"*Delivered*? Wow. By who? Take away?"

"My aunt's cleaner cooks for me."

"What? Every night?"

45

"Yeah. So?"

"You mean you can't cook yourself?"

"No. So?"

Sushila shrugged. "So nothing. So. Want to come and eat with us?"

I shook my head. "Nah. Not hungry," I said. It wasn't strictly true but I knew that Sushila had friends and if it was her birthday they'd probably be there at her house and I'd end up feeling spare or saying something stupid and putting my foot in it. "So no thanks."

"Whatever. Later then…" She went towards the front door to leave.

I wanted to kick myself. Why hadn't I taken up her offer? Was I mad? Rosa wouldn't know if I didn't eat her meal.

"Hey Sushila," I called. "If today's your birthday, you must be a Sagittarius like me right?"

"Yeah," said Sushila turning back. "Half man, half horse or something like that."

I nodded. "The archer with the horse's body. Yeah. That's the symbol for Sagittarians. Come and take a look at this… er that is if you've got time?"

Sushila smiled. "Sure."

I led her back into my room and turned on the computer and went to the astrological website. I thought I'd been a bit prissy turning down her offer of a meal so in order to appear more friendly, I thought I'd print out the page that said "Congratulations, you're this month's zodiac girl" when it came up.

The same night sky began to appear on the screen accompanied by the same spacey music then up popped the form.

"You have to fill in your details," I said.

"Cool," said Sushila sitting at my desk. She began to fill in her details. Date of birth, time, place.

When she'd finished, I waited for the strobe lights and the trumpets but instead the screen simply cleared then gave her horoscope and birth chart. No fanfare.

"Cool. Thanks. Can I print it out?" asked Sushila.

"Yeah. Sure." I pressed the print button and the papers began to swish out.

"You look puzzled," said Sushila. "What is it?"

"Just… when I did it, it kind of went mad. Said I was this month's Zodiac Girl. I thought it was because I'm Sagittarius, that all sagittarians are Zodiac Girls because it's our month."

"So do it again," said Sushila. "See if it does it again. It might have been that you were the thousandth person to enter the site or something and that made you Zodiac Girl or whatever."

"Oh yeah," I said. "I never thought of that. That's probably it."

I sat at the computer and went through the whole process of putting my birth date, place and time again.

The computer began to vibrate and once again came the trumpet and drum roll. *Really* loud.

Sushila laughed. "Wahoo. Hope you haven't got neighbours who like it quiet!"

"But what does it mean?" I asked.

"Dunno. You're this month's Zodiac Girl. Who knows? See if there's an email address and you can ask whoever runs the site. Whatever. Look. Sorry. Got to go. People waiting."

I let her out of the flat and when I closed the door after her, I spotted the package from Joe in the hall. *Good job he realized that the phone was mine*, I thought as I ripped the package open. Anyone might have picked it up and gone off with it.

Joe had wrapped the phone in bubble wrap and when I finally had it unwrapped, I realized that it wasn't my phone after all. He'd made a mistake. It was a lovely looking phone, a deep red colour with an amber stone encased in it but not mine. I went to my jacket to check if my phone was in there. I felt in the pocket and there it was where I always kept it. I'd been sure I hadn't left it in the café and I'd been right. *Never mind*, I thought. I could always take the red phone back to the deli one night after school and give it back to Joe.

I put it on the hall table and was about to go back into the living room to watch some telly.

Just as I put the phone down, it rang. It made me jump as it had a strange ring tone. In fact, hardly a ring tone at all. More like the trumpet fanfare that had announced that I was Zodiac Girl. At first I wasn't sure what to do. It wasn't my phone so I let it ring. *Surely it will click onto voice mail,* I thought and sure enough, after a few moments, the fanfare died down.

Then it started again. A few decibels louder. This time there was a loud thump on the wall from next door. The phone ring was loud enough to wake the dead.

Maybe I ought to pick up, I thought. *Maybe whoever's on the other end of the phone needs to get in touch with the owner of the phone so I ought to let them know that it has been misplaced in case it's an emergency. And whoever was on the end of the phone would obviously know who they were calling so I could ask who it belonged to so I could tell Joe when I handed it in. Yes,* I decided. *I'll answer the phone.*

"Hello."

"Hey Danu," said a friendly voice.

"How...? Who is this?"

"Joe."

"Joe from Europa?"

'The same."

"Hey Joe. Listen. This isn't my phone. Someone else must have left it in your cafe."

"No. It's yours."

"No. It isn't."

"Did you look at the site?"

"Yes."

"So you know you're this month's Zodiac Girl?"

"Er yeah… whatever that means."

"It means that this is your phone. Use it when you need help."

"Help?"

"Yes."

"From who? You mean like the emergency services?"

"No. Help from me."

"From you? You mean like if I need a take away? Oh that's brilliant. Thank you so much. I thought it was some kind of business promotion. Yeah. Thanks."

"No. That's not it at all. It's not so that you can order take away. I meant that you can get help from me. Joe."

"But why would I want help from you?"

"Because I'm your guardian. One month only. Special offer. Joe for Jupiter. That's me. Jupiter rules Sagittarius."

He's quite clearly deranged, I thought. *Harmless but deranged.* I decided to try and humour him. "I… I'm sure that's very kind but I can't afford a guardian or whatever…"

Joe laughed. "No cost. Free service. Because you're this month's Zodiac Girl."

"But I already have a guardian. My Aunt Esme."

"Aunt Esme. Yes. Good," said Joe. "Bring her with you one day to the deli. But seriously, we're different sorts of guardians. Call me whenever you need help. And keep checking into the site. I'll put a list of all the signs and their ruling planets on there so you can see that I'm not making it up. All the planets are here in human form you know."

"What?" *Definitely quite mad,* I thought.

"Yeah. Human form. But enough for now. All will be revealed. And in case you try to call anyone else on the phone, you can't. Only me."

And with that, he hung up.

I went back to my computer and uploaded the site. A huge arrow appeared pointing to a list on the right-hand side.

"Birth signs and their ruling planets," it read.

I pushed my mouse over to it then scrolled down:

Sign	Ruled by
Aries	Mars
Taurus	Venus
Gemini	Mercury
Cancer	Moon
Leo	Sun

Virgo	Mercury
Libra	Venus
Scorpio	Pluto
Sagittarius	Jupiter
Capricorn	Saturn
Aquarius	Uranus
Pisces	Neptune.

Okay, right. Interesting, I thought. A list of star signs and their ruling planets. But Joe had said that he *was* Jupiter and my guardian. *Was* Jupiter. And that all the planets were here in human form. I chuckled to myself. What a nutter. I'd heard of people thinking mad stuff like they were Napoleon or a chicken or something but I'd never come across someone thinking that they were a planet before. *Wow. All respect to him,* I thought. *It's amazing that being so barmy, he's managed to keep his deli going!* .

Chapter Five
Nits

"Year Nine will see the nurse first period then Year Eight after break," Mrs Richards announced at school assembly.

"What's happening?" I asked Sushila as I took my place in line. I was late for school because my curiosity had got the better of me and I'd taken another peek at the astrology site to see if there were any messages on there for me as Zodiac Girl. Sadly there was nothing very exciting, only my birth chart and my horoscope so I printed them off and had a quick look on the bus on the way to school.

Zodiac Girl's horoscope: An alignment between Uranus and Jupiter last Saturday led to surprise events.

Monday: a day for glorious rebellion – go for it.

Tuesday: the Moon moves into Cancer causing confusion.

Jupiter is in an expansive mood and brushes your chart with possibilities should you choose to take them.

Birth chart: Sagittarius Sun, Cancer rising, Moon in Taurus...

There were pages and pages. Some made a bit of sense – that Sagittarians are known for their big mouths and for being spontaneous and sporty and that they hate being hemmed in. They prefer roaming about outdoors and having adventures. *True, true, true*, I thought. And Cancer rising meant that I would be home loving and that although I might present a hard exterior, inside I was a big softie. Also true, but there were other parts of the birth chart that I didn't understand – that Saturn was square to Mars and the Moon was conjunct with Jupiter in the third house. I don't like not understanding things and I like a challenge so I had tried to decipher it. This made me late getting to the bus stop hence I'd got to school after the first bell and missed half of our headmistress's announcement. Not that I cared. Today could be my last day at the school if all went well and being late was a part of my plan to get myself thrown out.

"Nits," said Sushila. She took a look at my dreadlocks then stepped back. "We all have to see the nit nurse. She's going to have fun with your mop isn't she?"

I rolled my eyes. "Not my idea of a fun way to start the day." But not even the nit nurse could ruin the good mood I was in. I had a bag full of tricks from Uri's shop to try out and couldn't wait to get started.

The nurse put her comb into my hair and tugged it in an attempt to drag it through.

"Ow," I yelped putting my hands up to grab her wrists. "You're *hurting*."

Nurse Torturer shook my hands off and narrowed her eyes. "Tough. It's your own fault for having this peculiar hair. It's impossible," she said as she yanked at my head again. "I can't get the comb through. It's one big knot."

"It's not meant to be combed," I said.

Nurse T gave me a withering look which I think was supposed to scare me into submission but I stared right back at her. I was thinking, I must remember that expression and practise it at home. Purse the mouth, flare the nostrils slightly, narrow the eyes, frown and bingo, you have an excellent withering look. Nurse T's example was effective. She was intimidating and a half. Tall and bony with wiry grey hair and thin skin through which you could see the blue veins inside pulse with her blood. And she stank of disinfectant. Not one to be messed with.

"It's not meant to have nits either," she said, "but unless I can get this comb through, I can't be sure whether you have them or not. So young Madam.

What do you suggest?"

"That you leave me alone. Can't we leave it? I'm sure I haven't got nits."

"Not an option. I have a job to do."

"I'd know if I had nits," I said. "I'd feel them."

"Not necessarily."

"Well even if I do have nits, I don't want you to kill them. It's cruelty to animals. I'll report you to the NSPCA. Nit killer."

Nurse T gave me an exasperated look. "Listen kid, I have hundreds of pupils to see today. So here's the deal. Either you comb out your hair or I'll have to cut it off. The choice is yours but I will be back to check on you, you can count on that."

"You can't make me cut my hair!"

"Try me. I'll be back next week and either your hair is combed out so that I can get my comb through it or the lot comes off."

"I'm going to report you to the Head," I said.

"You do that," she said. "But not before I send you to see her myself.

"You do that," I said.

Great, I thought as I got up to leave. I'd love to get sent to the Head again. All part of the plan and soon Dad would have no choice but to let me go back home. I couldn't wait as actually it was beginning to get boring acting tough and defiant all the time. It's not me normally. I like learning. And I like doing well at school so it went against the grain to always be disinterested in class and not do my homework properly so that I got bad marks. I didn't want it to go on too long, like months or years or anything as I need to get good results in the end so that I can get the job I want. I'm still not sure what career I want but it will be either a travel writer, a foreign ambassador or a dancer on a pop music show on TV. Although you don't need mega qualifications for the last one, you do for the first two and I didn't want to mess up my chances in the long run by this bad girl act that I was having to pull. The sooner my plan worked, the quicker I could get back into ensuring my school CV was up to scratch.

When I'd finished with the nit nurse, I sneaked into the teacher's cloakroom and left the dirty face soap on one of the sinks. Then I reached up and took the mirror off its hook behind the door and stashed it in the end cubicle. With no mirror to check their appearance, any teacher who used the soap wouldn't know that their skin had changed colour until it was too late.

I made sure that I hung about near the cloakroom in the break so I could see if anyone went in and used the soap. I couldn't believe my luck. A hat trick of teachers went in. One, two, three. First Miss

Hardman went in and came out with dirty hands. I ducked round a corner but needn't have worried as she seemed preoccupied and in a rush and hadn't noticed that her hands had turned deep blue.

"What are you doing here, Jones?" Mr Beecham asked creeping up behind me and causing me to jump.

"Oh nothing…"

"On your way then, on your way…"

He went into the cloakroom and came out two minutes later with normal-coloured hands. *Hhmf*, I thought. *He doesn't wash his hands. Yuk.*

Next was Mrs McPhiblin. She came from the direction of the chemistry labs and spent a good five minutes in the cloakroom. *Result!* I thought when she came out with dark blue blotches all over her cheeks.

"And what pray is so amusing Miss Jones?" she said when she saw me peeking out from behind the lockers with a big grin on my face.

"Oh nothing," I said. "Just…"

A couple of Year Seven's went past and stared at Mrs McPhilbin's face then burst out laughing. She was beginning to get worried.

"What is it? Have I got something on my face?"

"Um. Only a nose like the rest of us," I replied.

At that moment, Mr Beecham came out of the staff room. "Good heavens, Madeleine," he said when he saw Mrs McPhilbin. "Your face! Your *face!*"

He ushered her into the staff room from where an anguished cry arose a few moments later. *My work is done!* I thought as I took off down the corridor. *They must have a mirror in there.*

Mr Beecham came hurtling after me not long afterwards. "Danu. *Danu.* Was that something to do with you?" he asked.

I wasn't going to deny it as it was all part of my plan to be as annoying as possible. "Yes. It was a special soap from the Black Sea. Good huh?"

"Get to your lesson and see the Head at lunch time," he said.

"Yes, sir," I said. "Thank you, sir."

He looked at me as if I was mad but I smiled back. Everything was working out brilliantly.

On the way to Maths, I took a quick detour to the swimming area. *Oh bat poo,* I thought when I saw that there were a number of people in there using the pool. At the far end in the little office, I caught sight of Mr Doherty, the swimming instructor, reading a paper. I ran over.

"Fire drill sir," I said breathlessly. "Headmistress sent me over to ask you to get everyone out in the next five minutes."

"But there was no bell," said Mr Doherty. "We'd have heard it."

"There was everywhere else sir. That's why I was

sent to get you. It's clearly not working over here but Mrs Richards says for you to get everyone out even if they're still in their swimming things and that she'll send someone afterwards to look at why the bell isn't working here."

Mr Doherty sighed heavily. "Nuisance, nuisance." He stepped outside his office and blew loudly on his whistle. "Right everyone. Out of the pool and into the playground. Fire drill."

A loud moan came from the swimmers but they did what they were told and begrudgingly got out of the pool, grabbed their towels and headed out in the direction of the playground.

Five minutes later, the pool area was empty. I reached into my rucksack and pulled out a bottle of superdye. *Lovely*, I thought as I poured the purpley-brown liquid into the pool. It began to work immediately, slowly seeping into the water and turning it a lovely bright red that began to spread all the way from the shallow to the deep end. *If my old mates could see me now, they'd die,* I thought because at my other school they used to tease me and call me Miss Goody Two Shoes. Now here I was being as bad as bad could be. And I had to admit, I was enjoying every minute of it.

The next lesson was Maths and I'd already been in and done my preparations when the others were lining up for the nit nurse. I'd taped the sound part of my remote-control fart machine under Mr Nash's chair.

I took my place with everyone else and the lesson soon got underway. As soon as Mr Nash sat down on his chair, I pressed the remote control from under my desk and a loud *thhhhhwwppppp* noise erupted from the front of the class.

Mr Nash looked around but of course, there was no-one behind his chair or anywhere near it. I pressed the button again. Another *thwppppppp* blasted from his chair and the class started laughing as Mr Nash stood up to try and see where the noise was coming from.

I repeatedly pressed the remote control from under my desk. *Thwrwp. Thwrwp. Thwrwp.* By now, everyone in the class was laughing their heads off. It was funny too because, try as he might, Mr Nash couldn't work out where the sound was coming from as there was no whoopee cushion or anything he could actually see.

He stood at the front of the class and glared at us. "One of you horrible lot is responsible for this. Now are you going to own up or do I give all of you detention?"

In way of a reply, I pressed the remote one more time. *Thwwppppp.* Everyone cracked up again.

Mr Nash continued to glare at us so I put my hand up.

"It was me, sir." And I demonstrated how it worked. "Brilliant, isn't it? The man in the shop said it works as far as fifty feet away so we could even use it on someone in another class."

Mr Nash sighed. "Harvey Jones. I might have known. Off with you now before I strangle you. I don't want you in my sight another moment. Go and see Mrs Richards *right* now."

I saluted him. "Yes, sir. Thank you, sir. Although I already have an appointment to see her at lunch time, I'm sure she won't mind me dropping in earlier as well." I went to the classroom door then turned back. "Maybe I should take the machine with me so that she can see how it works?"

The idea of this clearly appealed to most of the class and a few nodded but Mr Nash's expression let me know that he didn't agree so I shrugged.

"No? Okay then, later," I said and gave the class a little wave over my shoulder as I left.

What a great morning, I thought as I sauntered down the corridor waving through the glass partitions at anyone who could see me. I could get to like being bad.

Mrs Richards was furious. I suppose it didn't help that I gave her my exploding pen when she couldn't find her own pen to take notes.

"The swimming pool. The soap. The…" She couldn't bring herself to say fart machine, "*the…* rude noise machine, the pen. What next Danu?"

"Not sure," I said as I crossed my legs and looked thoughtful. "I've got itching powder, fake dog poo, I thought I might put that in a pan of the school dinners… um… a hand buzzer. Superglue. Fake blood capsules… so loads of stuff really. What do you think?"

Mrs Richards took a few deep breaths and regarded me calmly for a few moments. I almost lost my nerve because like Nit Nurse, she can do an impressive scary look, but suddenly her expression softened.

"I'm not a fool, Danu," she said gently. "And neither are you. Nor are you a pupil known for their bad behaviour at least not until you came here. So. I take it that these activities of yours are to provoke some sort of reaction. Am I right?"

I nodded. "Maybe."

"And what reaction would that be exactly?"

"I think you ought to give me the worst punishment there is. I think I ought to be expelled."

Mrs Richards pushed the palms of her hands together and studied me over them. "Oh you do, do you?"

I nodded. "Most definitely. My behaviour has been unacceptable. Totally out of order."

"Unacceptable? Hhmmm. Out of order? And if I say no?"

"I've still got my superglue, stink bombs…"

Mrs Richards sat and stared at me for a good few minutes before she spoke. "Are you *threatening* me, Danu?" she finally asked.

By this point, I really was starting to feel nervous. "No. Yes. I mean… I just think you should expel me."

"I think we both know that is not an option Danu. I spoke to your father before you started here. Where do you think that you would go?"

"Back to my old school."

Mrs Richards shook her head. "Danu, I'm sorry that your life has been disrupted. I know it can't have been easy but this mad behaviour of yours has to stop right now. Do you hear me? I'm not going to expel you. No. I'm not. But I will write to your father and let him know what's been going on. And I will see your aunt to discuss your attitude. In the meantime, you will see the school counsellor. Understood? In this school, *I* set the agenda, not the pupils and we don't give in to demands like yours. So you will not be getting your way. Understood?"

"Mfff," I muttered. "Understood."

I felt totally deflated. Angry that my plan hadn't worked. Frustrated that I was still going to be stuck here. And sad because it meant that I was destined to carry on living in my aunt's boring horrible flat.

When I got back out onto the corridor, my phone began to play its trumpet fanfare. I answered it as fast as I could as I didn't want to get called back into Mrs Richard's office. The screen told me that there was a text waiting for me so I opened up the message box and read:

"Grant me the serenity to accept the things I cannot change, the courage to change the things I can, and the wisdom to know the difference."

(by Reinhold Niebuhr)

Pffff, I thought as I glanced over it. *What would anyone with a name like Reinhold know? And anyway, I don't know anyone with that name. Some idiot must have sent the message to the wrong phone.*

Chapter Six
Bonkerooney Land

As I waited at the bus stop, I could see a few girls from school watching me and whispering behind their hands. Tales of my exploits had spread through the corridors like the Asian flu and I couldn't blame anyone for talking about me. I'd have been discussing the fact that someone had caused the swimming pool to turn bright red too if I had any friends. Which I don't.

As I stood at the stop trying to look cool, my zodiac mobile began to play its strange little tune again. Any image of looking indifferent went right out of the window as it blew its trumpet fanfare and a couple of people in the line behind me sniggered. *Probably a wrong number again*, I thought as I checked the message box again but no, this time there was a text message from Joe.

"Hey Danu. Zodiac Girl. Jupiter is in an expansive mood," it said. "Come to tea!"

Not a bad idea, I thought as I didn't relish going back

to the empty flat the way I was feeling. Plus I had to rethink my escape plan. So okay, Joe liked to think he was a planet, so what? My mate Fran used to talk to an imaginary friend when she was little, Bernie used to have long conversations with her cat and Annie used to think that she was a princess who had been stolen by gypsies and sold to people who pretended to be her parents. Everyone has their fantasies and the deli was safe enough. It was a public place. It wasn't like I was doing something stupid like going to meet a stranger somewhere isolated. And I was hungry. *No better location to rethink my plan*, I decided as I crossed to the other side of the road to the bus stop for Osbury.

Joe was delighted to see me and I was glad I'd made the detour. Even though I'd only met him recently, I felt like I'd found a new friend and it felt good to have a smiling face to greet me at the end of the day as opposed to an empty silent flat.

"So how was school today?" he asked as he placed a big mug of hot cocoa and fresh pancakes with maple syrup and bananas in front of me.

"Disaster," I said. "And I'd looked at your site this morning. It said it was a day for being rebellious and to go for it – but it didn't get me anywhere."

"Where did you want it to get you?"

I decided to tell him the truth. I was tired of

playing the tough girl who didn't care about anything. "Home, Joe. I want to go home *really* badly. I don't belong where I am. It's horrible and I want my old life back."

Joe sat down opposite me. "Ah. Change. Nothing as certain and nothing as uncertain."

I hadn't a clue what he meant. "Is that some kind of riddle?"

"Not really. There is nothing as certain to happen in life as change. Everything is changing, all the time. Nothing stays the same, does it? The weather, the news, the seasons, the leaves on the trees, the days of the week, every cell of your body in fact."

"So?"

"So sometimes the changes come from within us. We choose them, like a new hairstyle or a purchase or a decision to change the décor of a room. We control them to a certain extent. Sometimes, they come from outside. We don't control them. Like an earthquake or a train accident, not our choice at all. Know what I mean?"

I nodded. "I guess. I didn't choose the change that happened in my life. That's for sure. It was decided for me."

"And that's the uncertain bit," continued Joe. "Change can make us all feel uncertain. Especially the kind which we don't choose. Like, we have no control and fear what's going to happen next. But you know what? Sometimes things change for a reason. To move us on. To help us grow and further our journey. It doesn't always feel like that at the time, I know."

"Well I feel like my journey has gone backwards. I can't possibly learn anything where I am. Nothing happens there. The only books at Aunt Esme's flat are a telephone directory and the A-Z. I love books and my old house was full of them, in every room. And I have no-one to talk to. I feel like I'm living in a vacuum. I just wish I could be back home as things used to be."

"It won't be the same there you know. Things will have changed there too, with your old friends, with your old home, your old school. That will have moved on also. Nothing and nobody escapes change."

"Maybe. But at least I felt I belonged there. People knew me and cared about me."

"You have me now," grinned Joe. "Guardian for a month. I will help. Help you to think big!"

I didn't want to hurt his feelings so I smiled back. "Yeah. Right. That. I guess. It's not quite the same as having my dad or Mrs Wilkins our old housekeeper or my mates around though."

Joe looked sympathetic. "I know. I know." Then his face split into a grin again. "Know what Jupiter means?"

"It's the planet of jollity and expansion isn't it?" I knew that because I'd looked it up in the library in the afternoon break at school.

Joe nodded. "But the word, it's from the Greek, *Diu Pater*. Jupiter. God father. I'm like your godfather."

"If you say so Joe," I said.

"Well you don't look too pleased."

"Sorry. Just it's been a hard day. Nothing turned out how I'd hoped and now I feel I'm stuck."

"Ah. But life is what you make it Danu. Like the saying, if life gives you lemons, make lemonade."

To Joe's bemusement, I laughed. "Actually I *could* do that," I said. "Lemons are one of the few things Aunt Esme actually has in her fridge! She never buys any food or cooks or does any of the normal things that make a home a home."

"Then there's a place to make a start. Make lemonade. You like lemonade?"

I nodded.

"So make some," said Joe. "This is what you have to learn, Danu my friend. You get my text before?"

"About coming for tea? Yes."

"No. The one before that."

"The one from Reindeer Nebu or someone?"

"Reinhold Niebuhr. 'Grant me the serenity to accept the things I cannot change, the courage to change the things I can, and the wisdom to know the difference.'"

"I thought that was a mistake. Sent to the wrong phone."

"No, I sent it. To make you think. Listen Danu, if you're not happy with the hand that fate has dealt you, then do something about it. You have two choices. Sulk or smile. Sink or swim."

"That's four choices…"

"But you know what I mean," said Joe.

"But I *have* been trying to do something. I've been trying to get expelled and then I can go home."

"Okay," said Joe. "Let's start there. Home. It sounds important to you."

"Is. Was."

"That's because you have a lot of Cancer in your birth chart."

"Yeah. I saw that. Cancer rising. But I thought I was Sagittarius."

"You are," said Joe. "Your Sun sign is Sagittarius but your rising sign is Cancer."

"Don't understand," I said.

"There's a lot more to astrology than being one sign. Yes, you have a Sagittarius Sun sign but you are also affected by where the Moon was when you were born, where Venus was, Neptune, all the planets. There are ten of them and they all affect your chart in different ways. You have a strong Cancerian influence in yours. Home is very important to

Cancers which is why you won't have liked being uprooted."

"Tell me about it," I said as I sipped my hot chocolate.

"Well, as a Sagittarian, you like space. It's the sign that most likes space around them so if you're cooped up in a small flat, it's no wonder you've been finding it difficult."

"Too right. That's why I want to go back to my old house. There was plenty of space there."

"What happened to it?" asked Joe.

"Rented out to a new family."

"So you can't go back there can you?"

I shook my head. "I guess not. But there have to be other options."

"There are *always* other options," said Joe. "Always. So okay, let's look at them."

"Okay."

I was beginning to like Joe more and more. He was the first grown-up in ages who had actually taken me seriously. He seemed to understand why I was unhappy and was listening to what I had to say.

"So home," he said. "Important. Right. What made your home a home?"

"It was where my pets were and they were always happy to see me when I came back from school or anywhere. There were always people round. There was always the smell of baking. It felt warm. There were books around. We had a great garden. Fresh flowers on the table. And even though Dad wasn't there a lot of the time, I knew he was around somewhere."

"Right. Good," said Joe. "So. Let's think. Which of these elements do you think that you can bring to where you are now?"

"Um. None. Not really. I can't keep my pets there. They need to get out into a garden and anyway, they have new owners now."

"What about new pets?" asked Joe.

"Still need to get out into a garden. It's not fair otherwise."

Joe nodded. "Except goldfish. You could get some fish."

"I guess. But… Um… No… It's very much my aunt's flat and I somehow don't think she'd like it. She likes the minimal look, nothing on the walls, no nick-nacks, no pictures, definitely no fish! The flat smells… clinical somehow, like a hospital, not a cosy smell at all."

"Does she spend much time in the flat?"

"Nope."

"Hhmm," said Joe. "Maybe she doesn't find it very homely either. Maybe *she'd* like to see someone who's pleased to see her when she comes home. How do you greet her?"

I thought back to most times when she came home. Usually I was in bed asleep or I just grunted at her from the sofa. Not an especially welcoming hello. But then, she wasn't exactly Miss Happy-to-See-You when she came in. Usually she had something critical to say before I'd even had the chance to say, hi, good morning or evening or whatever. I guess we both had a lot to learn.

"Okay. Let's go back to the basics," continued Joe. "You said something about the smell of cooking. Smells of baking. Yes. I like those too. How about you create some of those yourself? Learn how to cook. I can give you a stash of easy recipes." He got up and went to rummage around behind the counter from where he produced a pile of papers.

"Here. Recipes. For you to try."

"*Me*? Cook? Never."

"Have you ever tried?"

"Not really."

"There you go then. You've given up before you've even tried. So that's your choice. Loser."

"Loser? You're calling *me* a loser?"

Joe nodded. "Yeah. Loser. Given up before you've tried. The one thing you *could* change but you, yes, *you,* have chosen not to."

"But I'm only thirteen."

"So? Where in the rule book does it say that you

have to be a certain age to cook? Anyway, you're thirteen *next* birthday. I've seen your chart. You're an adventurer. You're curious. You could probably be an excellent cook. Give it a go. What's your favourite meal?"

"You mean like my death meal?"

Joe looked puzzled. "Death meal?"

"Yes. If you knew it was to be your very last meal on earth and you didn't have to worry about calories or cholesterol or all the other stuff adults worry about, what would it be?"

"Easy. For me, lasagne with extra cheese and homemade vanilla ice cream with raspberry sauce."

"Good choice," I said.

"But it was supposed to be *me* asking you what you liked," laughed Joe. "So, what's your death meal?"

"Chips. Big chunky ones. And mayo to dip them in. And chocolate muffins, like Mrs Wilkins used to make. God, I miss her cakes. She was a star. Carrot cake. Banana. Vanilla. Almond."

"Poor Danu. No cakes. Oh woe is me, poor poor little me," groaned Joe.

"Well it hasn't been easy..." I began and then realized that he was teasing me.

"Hmmf," said Joe. "I am afraid I have no sympathy at all. You could have been eating Mrs Wilkins cake every night if you wanted and treating your aunt to some as well. Instead you've been moping about like a mopey moping thing. Pathetic. But… your choice, your choice."

"Hey! If you're my godfather, aren't you supposed to be *nicer* to me?"

"I am being nice. This *is* being nice. I'm saying there's a lot about your life that you could change. Starting with cakes. You're too thin, you should eat more. You like nice cakes. *You* bake them. You're not stupid. What's stopping you?"

I felt a knot of rage in the pit of my stomach rise to my throat. *You don't understand*, I thought but then I got an image of myself as the mopey moping thing that Joe had spoken about and the feeling of anger evaporated. I couldn't think of a single reason not to do what he suggested. What he'd said had really got through to me. My choice. Sulk or smile. Sink or swim and I could add another, starve or cook. Yeah. I could do that. It would give me something to do as well. Yeah. I'd even write to Mrs Wilkins for her recipes. Yes. It would be a start at least. I might even bake something for grumpy old Aunt Esme.

When Joe went over to his counter to serve a few more customers, I glanced over the recipes he'd given me. *I might not have to write to Mrs Wilkins,* I thought as I read over them. The ones he'd given me seemed easy enough.

After a while Joe came back over.

"See those two over there?" he asked.

I glanced over at a man and woman who had come in and were sitting at the window table. She was tall and glamorous with long blonde hair and he had the look of a young handsome poet with a shoulder-length mane of wavy dark hair. Both had something about them, an energy that made you want to stare.

"Yeah."

"Venus and Mercury. Remember what I was telling you about all the planets being here in human form?"

Oh God, I thought. *He's gone off into Bonkerooney Land again and just as we were getting along so nicely and I was beginning to think that he was half sane.* I decided it was best to humour him and go along with it.

"Okay, yes," I said. "Those two over there are Venus and Mercury?"

Joe nodded. "It's important that you understand. You have grasped that each sign has a ruling planet, haven't you?"

"Yeah." I pulled out the list he'd sent me that I'd printed with my horoscope. "Here's the list."

"And you understand that the ruling planet is like a guardian."

"Yeah. Godfather, *Diu Pater*, guardian," I said. "Yeah. Sort of, if you want to put it that way."

Joe's expression was serious and he sighed. "No

Danu. I think you are humouring me. Thinking crazy man. I don't think you're really getting it."

"Not getting what?"

"That the guardians are *here*, on this planet."

I couldn't hold it in any longer and I burst out laughing. "Sorry, sorry Joe. But it *does* sound mad. What you're saying is that the aliens are amongst us. I mean, *hello*, Planet Earth to Jupiter. I think you've been watching the scifi channel too much."

Joe looked put out. "I don't watch TV. I'm telling you the truth. I told you, you have to think big Danu."

"Okay. And how does anyone recognise these guardians then? Do they have, like, a secret handshake?"

"Many don't ever get to meet their guardian. Only those chosen to be Zodiac Girls. And even some of them choose to ignore it."

And I can see why, I thought.

Joe looked dejected as if I'd hurt his feelings.

"You're serious, aren't you Joe?"

"Of course."

"And you're my guardian?"

"Yep. I've *told* you. Jupiter for Sagittarius."

"You're telling me that you're the living manifestation of the planet Jupiter and that you run a deli."

He nodded. "That's the truth, Danu."

I was determined not to laugh again as he looked so earnest and I didn't want to tread on his feelings no matter how crazy they were. He was clearly harmless and very well meaning.

"So… Okay. So what do the others do?"

"That's what I'm trying to tell you," said Joe. "That couple over there. She's Nessa. Manifestation of Venus. He's Hermie. Manifestation of Mercury."

"Hermie for Hermes, messenger god?"

"That's right," said Joe. "Yep. He's my son, actually. Hermie or Mercury. Greeks called him Hermes, others call him Mercury. He works for a company called Mercury Communications as a motorbike messenger boy."

I was having a hard time holding it together. "And don't tell me, Nessa runs the fish-and-chip shop."

Joe guffawed loudly causing a couple of people to look over. "No! Don't be ridiculous."

I breathed a sigh of relief. He had been teasing me. He didn't believe any of it after all.

"*Neptune* runs the chippie," Joe continued. "I think you met him briefly. Old geezer with the white beard? Can be a bit of a grump."

Oh bat poo. Joe really did believe what he was saying. *Poor man,* I thought, *clearly A1 bonkers.*

"Okaaaaay," I said. "So Neptune runs the chippie. Um… let's pick another from the list. Here. Aquarius ruled by Uranus. So what does Uranus do?"

"Uri. You met him. Runs the magic shop."

Wow, Joe may be from Bonkerooney Land but he has a vivid imagination, I thought.

I glanced back at my list. "And Pluto rules Scorpio. So Pluto?"

"Interior designer," replied Joe. "Stylist. Does makeovers. Transformations, that sort of thing."

"Saturn?"

"Ah Saturn. The great taskmaster. Teaches you some major lessons in life does Saturn. He's a headmaster. Dr Cronus."

"Moon?"

"Oh I'll let you find out that for yourself," said Joe. "In fact, if I remember your chart right, you have an encounter with her coming soon."

"Marvellous," I said as I got up to go. "Can't wait."

Time to go home, I thought. So. Saturn was a headmaster and Neptune ran the chippie. That confirmed it. Joe was mad. Completely mad. But his being mad suddenly gave me an excellent idea to try out at school…

Chapter Seven

Psycho woman

Tuesday lunch time and it was my appointment to see the school counsellor. I was well ready. Plan A hadn't worked but Plan B had begun to hatch in my brain on the way home last night after seeing Joe.

It's your choice how your life turns out, he'd told me. Okay, I told myself. My number one option was still to get out of here and unknowingly, by ordering me to see the school counsellor, Mrs Richards had presented me with a way to do it. I was going to pretend that I was stark staring bonkers. Flies in the attic. Spanner in the head or whatever. Mad. I was going to get myself dismissed on grounds of being mental. If that didn't bring my dad hurrying back from the graveyard slot, I didn't know what would.

I sat outside the counsellor's office going over my act. I would be a little snuffly and occasionally make weird bird-like noises. I would make my eyes go cross-eyed. I'd let one arm have a life of its own and float up in the air above my head. And I'd dribble.

If none of that worked, I'd pretend I was a teapot.

After about five minutes sitting there, running through what I hoped was to be an Oscar-winning performance, the school secretary came out.

"You can go in now Danu," she said. "Miss Luna will see you now. Door on the right."

"Umbanga," I said and beamed back at her.

She gave me a strange look so I winked at her and went into the door that she'd indicated.

"Oh!" I said when I got inside and saw the lady who was waiting for me. "Are you the counsellor?"

The lady who was standing by the window nodded her head slightly. She wasn't what I had imagined although I don't know what I'd expected. Someone who looked professional in smart clothes like a teacher or a bank manager or something. Not the woman who was in front of me. For a moment, I forgot to do my mad act as I was too busy gawping at her. She looked like an artist or a gypsy with long silver grey wavy hair, a crescent moon pendant round her neck, stars on her ears and she was wearing a silvery silk skirt that matched her hair. She looked like a waif mermaid who had grown legs and been washed ashore. I waited for her to say something so that I could begin my act but she didn't. She just stood staring out of the window up at the sky. After a while, when she hadn't taken any notice of me, I began to wonder if she even knew that I was there.

I coughed. "Ahem."

She turned to look at me then but still didn't say anything.

"I'm Danu. Your one o'clock. Raving loonie reporting for counselling. Yes, Ma'am." I saluted like they do in the army then began to bark like a dog.

No reaction. She just looked at me. Then put her arms out and began to sway, side to side, front to back. *What the bat poo is she doing?* I wondered. I let her carry on for a moment then she stopped and sat down. She looked as though she was going to cry.

I sat down opposite her. She reached out to the table, took a tissue and blew her nose.

"Well aren't you going to say anything?" I asked. "Take notes? Give me some advice?"

She sniffed. "No."

We sat there in silence for a while then my curiosity got the better of me.

"Um. Aren't you supposed to do something?" I asked. "Say something wise?"

She turned her silvery blue eyes in my direction. "What? What could *I* possibly say?"

"Dunno. But isn't it your job to *know* what to say or do?"

Her eyes filled with tears. "Say. Do. Is that all

there is? Sometimes all I want to do is *be*. It's best just to go with the flow." She rose from her chair and went to stand at the window where she tilted her face to look at the sky again. "You know Danu, sometimes I think *Is this it?* There has to be more. Otherwise what's it all been for?"

And then to my total and utter amazement, she started to dance. A flowy, hippie type of dance like the kind that we used to do when we were in junior school and some over-enthusiastic teacher would say, "Everyone be a tree, let your arms be branches and sway with the breeze why don't you?".

I watched her with my mouth hanging open for a few moments then the penny dropped. *Ah. Yes. I get it*, I thought. *She's trying to out-loon me. Yes, she's clever this one. She knows the stunt I was going to try and she's trying to outdo me. Well, hah! I sussed it and I'm not giving up here.*

I got up and joined in her wacko dancing. I could dance like a loonie petunie too. "Yes. Yes. Come on, let's be trees," I said as I waved my arms in the air and bent my knees. "Bending in the wind, this way, that way. La la la la la la laaaaaaaaa."

"Not trees," she said as she pranced around the room. "Water. Dance like the water, flowing, the tides go in, the tides go out. Go with the flow Danu, go with the flow."

She must have done some up-to-the-minute

counselling course where they teach this as a new approach to try with difficult pupils. *Fine by me*, I told myself as I followed her lead.

"Water. Flow. Right. Can do," I said and changed my tree dance to the sea dance which actually looked pretty similar and consisted of me wiggling my hips and waving my arms side to side in the air.

We danced round the room for a few minutes like a pair of demented hippies then she stood on one of the chairs. "If I stretch high enough, I can reach the stars."

Ohmigod, I thought when I realized that she was showing no signs of giving up either. *What if she really is bonkers? In fact...*

"Excuse me Miss but are you really the school counsellor?" I asked.

She looked down at me from the chair. "I am and I'm not. I don't think we ought to define ourselves by what we do. Do you? I mean, do you feel that you are just a schoolgirl."

"Blimey no. I'm much more than that."

"There you are then. So don't ask stupid questions."

"Right," I said and sat down to try and work out my next move.

Miss Luna finally got down off the chair and sat on the couch opposite me.

"So," she said.

At last, I thought. *She's done with trying to act madder than me and we're going to get down to business.* "So…"

And then she burst into tears. First a few sobs and then her chest began to heave… and heave. *Wow,* I thought. *This lady really is a psycho woman. She's not putting this on.*

I handed her the box of tissues. "Is there anything I can do Miss Luna? Shall I fetch someone?"

"Oh no, no." She carried on sobbing but took a tissue. "Please… please don't tell anyone… just I'm not feeling myself today… and please call me Selene not Miss Luna. That sounds so grown-up."

"Oh okay. Selene. I won't tell anyone. I promise. Now. Do you want to tell me what's wrong? It can't be all that bad."

Selene or Miss Luna lay back on the couch, flicked her shoes off and began to tell me all about how she felt, how it wasn't easy for her being so affected by the waxing or waning of the Moon.

"Every two days the Moon changes signs," she sobbed. "If it's not waxing, it's waning, then it's full, half moon then new moon, crescent. Never a day off to relax."

I had no idea what she was on about but I listened patiently. The more I listened, the gist of it seemed to be that she was having the same problem that I had.

She didn't like everything changing all the time either. I didn't know what to say but talking did seem to help her so I let her go on. Every now and then I would interject by saying, "Uhuh. And how do you feel about that?".

At the end of my hour, my "counsellor" had calmed down. She looked at her watch. "Oh time's up," she said. "Thank you so much. You've been marvellous. I feel... well, almost... more cheerful about things."

"Anytime," I said as I got up to leave. "Call me anytime you need to talk."

"Thank you sooooo much," said Selene. "I will."

And then it dawned on me. Tides. Waxing. Waning. Moons. Joe had told me I might have an encounter with the moon. He couldn't have meant Miss Luna could he?

"Hey, you don't by any chance know Joe Joeve who runs the deli do you?"

Selene nodded. "*Diu Pater*. Godfather. Of course. Everyone knows him round here."

"And er... you don't by any chance think you're the Moon do you?"

She laughed as if I'd said something really stupid then she nodded again. "Of course I do because that's who I am. But how did you know?"

"Joe told me that my horoscope said that I had an

encounter with the Moon today. I didn't know what he meant though. He's been telling me a lot of things I don't understand in fact."

Selene beamed at me. "Of course! You're a Zodiac Girl. You are, aren't you?"

"Zodiac Girl, Queen of Sheba or demented chicken. I'm still trying to decide."

Selene looked perplexed. "Pardon?"

"Okay," I said. "Um… put it this way, if you think you're the Moon, then yes, I'm a Zodiac Girl." *I wonder how many there are in their club*, I asked myself. What Joe had told me about people being planets was beginning to make sense. They obviously belonged to a club that was into astrology and each of them got a nickname when they joined – like you be the Moon, you be Mars, I'll be Venus – in the same way that anybody might like to dress up according to their favourite characters. My mate Jane was Harry Potter-mad and belonged to a club back home where all the members dressed up as characters from the books. Jane got to be Hermione Granger every second Saturday. So Joe, Miss Luna, Hermie and the others, they weren't mad. Maybe a little eccentric. That was all.

"I thought you were unusually perceptive," said Selene. "Most of the pupils here can't see what's in front of them. But you can. Yes. I should have known that you were a Zodiac Girl. Now everything makes more sense."

A little, I thought as I got up to leave. Miss Luna is another member of a strange club along with a load of others who like to pretend that they are planets. Why not? At least it made life more interesting and I did feel marginally better after my counselling session. Maybe Miss Luna's "dance like the sea" therapy had something going for it after all.

Chapter Eight

Cakes

What an insane day, I thought as I let myself into the flat after school. I went into the kitchen to put my supplies on the counter. I'd been having a big think about everything Joe had said to me at our last meeting – about how if you want a home, make it yourself. And the quote about knowing what you could change and what you couldn't had made more sense after talking to him. Once Joe had explained it, it seemed obvious and I didn't know why I hadn't thought it before. So, okay, maybe I couldn't change the fact that I had to live here a bit longer and I couldn't change the fact that I had to go to the new school, but I could change how it was living with Aunt Esme. I could make her cold unwelcoming flat more of a home and as Joe had suggested, I was going to start with a bit of baking. I'd been to Mr Patel's shop and bought all the ingredients I thought I'd need to make cakes. Chocolate cakes were my favourite so I'd bought a large bar of dark chocolate, butter, flour, sugar, milk, icing sugar, pecans and cherries.

I glanced over the recipe that Joe had given me and as directed switched the oven to 190C.

I laid out all my ingredients on the counter in the order that I'd need them then looked for a baking tray. Nothing. I went from cupboard to cupboard but there was little there: just a couple of plates, two bowls, three mugs, two wine glasses, two tumblers, one box of my breakfast cereal. I felt so disappointed as I'd been looking forward to my first attempt at being a super chef. I was about to turn off the oven when I spotted a drawer under the oven door. I pulled it open and luckily, there were a couple of baking tins and a baking tray in there. All pristine, never been used. *They must have come with the flat*, I thought. Aunt Esme would never go out and buy something you needed to cook with in a million years.

Another quick check of my supplies and I was off.

When Rosa arrived with my supper at six o'clock, she sniffed the air in appreciation.

"Making the cook?" she asked.

I nodded. "Cooking. Making the cakes. I am. Almost ready. Want to try?"

She shook her head as if she didn't understand so I acted out eating and pointed at the kitchen. She nodded her head.

My cakes were almost ready and I'd followed the

directions to the letter and judging by the lovely buttery cocoa smell, they were going to turn out fine. I could hardly believe how good the simple exercise of baking had made me feel. It reminded me of home when I used to help Mrs Wilkins. And the time had flown. Usually the hours when I got home from school were the worst, when I felt the most lonely, but this time, I'd been so busy, I'd hardly noticed being on my own.

Rosa came and stood by the kitchen door so I pointed at the oven, crossed my fingers and made an anxious face. She laughed and sniffed the air.

"Smell goods."

When the timer bell on the oven dinged, I opened the door and took out my tray of cakes. They had risen beautifully and looked perfect. Rosa did a little clap so I gave her a bow.

It was nice having someone in the kitchen. My second visitor in a week. I looked at Rosa and pointed at the kettle. "Cup of tea?"

She nodded and smiled. "Thanks to you."

I made us some tea and when the cakes had cooled, I put them on a plate and took them into the living room. Rosa followed me but seemed hesitant to sit.

"No, please," I said, indicating that she should sit down.

She sat on the edge of the sofa, took a cake and bit into it.

"Very very goods," she smiled at me.

I took one too and tried it. It was good. The dark chocolate had melted beautifully to make bursts of liquid chocolate in the middle. Delicious.

As we sat there munching, I realized that Rosa and I had never exchanged more than two or three words in all the time that she'd been coming. I'd been so cross with Dad and Aunt Esme that I'd taken it out on her too. But it wasn't her fault that I'd been left alone and as we sat there, I began to wonder what her life was like. She didn't speak much English so she must have felt alienated at times as well.

"Where do you live Rosa?" I asked. I pointed at her then acted out going to sleep.

"Ah," she replied. "Sleeping. I sleep..." she pointed out the window in the direction of the flats on top of Mr Patel's corner shop at the other side of the square.

"And your home?"

She looked at me quizzically.

"Home," I repeated. "Family. Are your family there?"

She didn't understand so I fetched my purse and got out the photo that was taken of Dad and me in the garden last summer. "Family. Me. Dad," I said.

Her face suddenly looked sad and she shook her head. "No. No family here. Family Poland."

I nodded. "You have friends here?"

"Cousin Halina. She nice lady. She work here too. No see much." She then pointed at me. "You? Family is where?"

"Mum died when I was three," I said but Rosa looked puzzled. "Dead. Caput." I acted out someone having their throat cut which she clearly didn't get. So I acted out someone being shot in the head which caused her to look even more confused. I lay on the floor with my eyes closed then acted out someone stabbing me with a knife. Rosa looked horrified.

"Murdering?" she asked.

I shook my head vigorously. Mum had been ill but she died peacefully in her sleep. *Maybe I should have thought of a more subtle way of acting out deceased*, I thought. Then I had an idea. I raced to my room and got a few sheets of paper. I drew a matchstick man getting on an aeroplane.

I pointed to the drawing and then the photo of Dad.

"Dad," I said and Rosa nodded.

Then I drew a matchstick lady under the ground with a cross above her. Rosa nodded. I think she got the fact that Mum wasn't here any more. And lastly, I drew a smaller man for my brother and showed him to be at a building by the sea reading a book. "Brother, university," I said.

"Understand. University," Rosa smiled then took the pen and paper. She drew a mother, father and three little girls. "Sisters," she said. Then she drew £££ signs and pointed to herself. "I work, send money."

I nodded. So she was away from her family too. I wondered what her life was like back in Poland and whether she missed her friends and family and if she had any pets. I drew a dog, cat and horse. She nodded and drew two cats. She looked sad when she drew them.

We looked at each other and I put my hand on my heart. She put her hand on hers. *We understand each other completely*, I thought, *even though we don't have all the words. She's lonely too.* I resolved to make time for her in future when she brought my supper. I'd been so selfish grumping about like a miserable brat when all the time she had been missing her home and family just like me.

After she'd gone, I cleared up the kitchen, left a cake out for Aunt Esme then went to my computer to check for mail. Only one from my brother who had finally remembered that I existed.

Hey Danu. Sorry I haven't been in touch. Let me know if you need anything. Look after yourself.

Luke.

Pff, I thought. Hopeless. He's as bad as Dad. Head in the clouds and nose in a book. He's studying ancient history and wasn't very interested in anything or anybody else.

I quickly did a round robin email to Annie, Fran, Bernie and Jane letting them all know what I'd been up to and as I was finishing up, my zodiac phone went.

"Hey Danu," said Joe. "Go to the site. There's a competition on there that's just up your street. First correct answer wins. And according to your chart, Pluto is coming square to your fourth house."

"D'oh. Which means what?"

"Oh right. Pluto is the planet of transformation and your fourth house is the house of home. So it sounds fated that you win doesn't it? Don't waste any time. Bye."

I went to the astrology site and just as Joe had said, a pop-up appeared inviting me to take part in a competition.

Answer this question and win a makeover for your home from top stylist PJ Vlasaova and his team of wonder workers.

Excellent, I thought, *Joe is really on the ball.* First his brill idea about baking and now this. If I win a home makeover, I could make a mark on this place and cheer it up a bit. And what's more, it could be a surprise for Aunt Esme.

I looked to see what the question was.

Dui Pater is another name for what?

Easy peasy, lemon squeezy, I thought as I typed in my answer: Jupiter.

Chapter Nine
Bad boys

School was uneventful for the rest of the week as I behaved myself for a change and kept my head down in class. I still haven't made any real friends there but people certainly know who I am now: the girl with the big mouth. The girl who cheeks the teachers. The girl who put trick soap in the teacher's cloakroom, turned the swimming pool bright red etc etc. But nobody knows who I really am behind the tough act. I'm still the lonely girl. I wished Sushila was in my class because even though she has loads of friends, she always stops to chat if she sees me in the playground or at the bus stop after school.

"Hey Danu," asked Marie Marshall who sits behind me in Maths. "Got any more good tricks up your sleeve?"

I shook my head. "Nah. That phase in my life is over."

"So what next?" she asked.

"Not sure," I replied. "I might stand for parliament

but I might also join the foreign legion. Whatever. You'll have to find someone else to entertain you when classes are dull."

Marie's face registered hurt for a second. "I was only asking," she said. "No need to be sarcastic."

The bell went and she flounced out to break with her friend. *Stupid, stupid,* I thought. Why had I snapped at her like that? She was only being friendly but I hadn't given her a chance. We could have had a nice normal chat about what I was going to do next. I was looking forward to it immensely. My "get myself expelled" plan hadn't worked. My "act like a mad person" hadn't worked. So I was ready to embark on Plan C. I was going to stop resisting and fighting against what had happened, I'd decided. I was going to go with the flow as Miss Luna would say (only without the hippie dancing). I'd try to accept the situation and make it better little by little. Joe had said it was up to me to make the changes and that's what I was going to do. Make some changes starting at the flat.

So far, it was all coming together beautifully. A couple of days after I'd entered the competition on the website, an email had come through saying that I'd won and the day after that, I got an email from the design team asking when I'd like them to come.

"Next Monday," I wrote back. "And it has to be

done in a week."

Aunt Esme was flying off to New York on Sunday evening. Rosa was coming to stay. We had the half term week to do the flat before she got back.

The timing couldn't have worked out better. I couldn't wait.

After school, I popped into the Patels' to get supplies for a carrot cake that I wanted to try out. I wanted to get home before the rain storm that had been threatening all afternoon began. Already the wind was whipping up making the square seem even colder and more unfriendly than usual. As I was walking towards our tower block with my purchases, I decided to call Joe to check something about the recipe. I pulled out my phone and punched in his code. Big mistake. A bunch of boys were hanging about near the ball sculpture in the middle on the square. One of them spotted my phone and nudged one of the others who looked my way. I could tell immediately that they were going to cause trouble.

"Hello, hello?" asked Joe at the other end of the phone. "Is that you Danu? Is everything all right?"

"Yes. No. Um. Got to go."

I quickly put the phone away. I should have known better. Our PSHE teacher was always warning us about keeping any items anyone might want to steal hidden when in dodgy places but too late, they had seen it.

One of the boys jutted his chin at one of the others and he glanced my way and then nodded. A feeling of sickness hit the pit of my stomach. They were going to try and get me. I could feel it. I quickly counted them. One, two, three, four, five. *Should I run back to the shop?* I wondered, *or try and make it up to the flat? Better decide.* The boys were coming towards me. *Oh God, oh God. So much for being a Zodiac Girl bringing me luck,* I thought. *My zodiac phone is just about to land me in it.*

I glanced over at the boys. They were getting closer. *Run or fight?* I asked myself as fear flooded through me. *Run, run,* said a voice in my head. But my feet weren't moving. Suddenly from somewhere, deep in my gut, my fear turned to anger. I'd had enough of feeling that life was against me. Abandoned by Dad. Ignored by Aunt Esme. Left out by the girls at school. Enough! I'd had enough and I wasn't going to take any more especially from a bunch of spotty-looking boys who were after the one nice present that anyone had given me in ages. *Fight,* said a voice at the back of my head.

I shoved the phone back deep in my pocket, leant on one hip and turned to the boys.

"Want something?"

"Yeah," sneered a tall boy with lank greasy hair. "Give us yer phone."

I gave him my best Nit Nurse withering look. "Give *me* your phone," I said. "Me, not us, and your, not yer. That's the correct way to say it you stupid boy. Now repeat after me. Give me *your* phone."

One of the boys sniggered which seemed to annoy the tall boy.

"Shuddit Bazza," he growled.

"Shut *it*," I said and looked around as if in exasperation. "Didn't anyone teach you boys to speak properly?"

For a moment the boys were stunned into silence. It looked as though nobody had ever spoken to them like I had and part of me couldn't believe my nerve. But it didn't take the tall boy long to regain his cockiness. He gave me a look like I was a piece of dirt then walked towards me and shoved my shoulder. "I said, give us yer phone."

I knew I was asking for trouble as the other thing that our PSHE teacher said is that if one of us is ever mugged or picked on, just hand over whatever it is that your assailant wants as your life is worth more than a watch or a phone or whatever's being stolen. I knew that it was true but I wasn't in a sensible mood. I felt angry and I wasn't going to take being pushed around. I tried shoving the boy back but two of his mates grabbed my wrists and held them back. By now, my heart was beating really fast and my earlier courage was beginning to fade. *Why oh why doesn't anyone like a policeman walk past when you need them?* I thought.

The ringleader reached for my pocket to try and grab my phone. I wiggled away so that he couldn't reach. He tried again. As my arms were pinned back, all I had to fight back with were my legs so I gave him a swift kick in the shin.

"Oww," he cried and bent down to rub his leg then he laughed an evil laugh, stood upright and looked at me as if he was deciding what to do with me next.

"Seems like we've got a fighter here, Trev," said the chubby one called Bazza to the tall boy as I kicked out again and struggled to get free. "A fighter with no brain."

Trev laughed again.

"It's you who's got no brain," I said. "You're pathetic picking on a girl on her own."

Trev looked around as if he was pleased with himself. "Er… I don't think so, little girl. Five of us. One of you. You do the maths."

"I have," I said. "And it adds up to COWARDLY."

The boy scowled and attempted to reach for my pocket again as I wiggled and squirmed and tried to get away from him. But it was no use. They were all closing in on me and I was getting weaker. I closed my eyes and felt the boy reach into my pocket and begin to pull out the phone. I was about to tell them to take the stupid phone and just leave me alone when suddenly I felt one of the boys being pulled off.

"I DON'T think that's yours, lad," said a familiar voice.

I opened my eyes. It was Joe. And boy did he look angry.

"Joe," I cried. I'd never been happier to see anyone in my whole life.

Joe bowed. "At your service Danu," he said.

Trev laughed. "At your service," he mimicked. "Yeah right old geezer. Get him lads."

The boys released me and lined up ready to attack Joe. My heart was pounding away in my chest by now and I could hardly breathe.

I leapt on Bazza's back. "You leave him alone," I said.

Bazza shrugged me off like he was discarding an unwanted jacket.

Trev laughed again. "Or else what?"

Oh God, I thought. *Or else what indeed?* There were only two of us and Joe was by no means young or fit-looking with his round belly.

But something was starting to happen to Joe.

He took a deep breath in and seemed to grow in stature. Like someone was pumping him up like a bicycle tyre. He grew and grew. His belly began to shrink and his stomach appeared flatter. His shoulders grew broader. He seemed to be growing younger by the second. And taller. And no, yes... he was sprouting a beard! I rubbed my eyes. *This can't be happening*, I thought as I watched Joe transform in front of my eyes into a lean mean fighting machine. *A lean mean fighting machine with... no, no way, I can't be seeing this!* I told myself. Joe's top half looked like that of a young athlete but his bottom half... his bottom half... *It can't be...* looked like that of a horse! *No. Not possible.* I rubbed my eyes again and felt like I was about to faint. I swooned back against the nearest wall to recover and catch my breath. At that moment, there was a loud boom of thunder, a crack of lightning and the skies began to pour. In the dim light, it was hard to see exactly what was going on, it was all happening so fast. *I must be imagining it*, I thought as I watched Joe or someone very like Joe flex his muscles and charge into the scrum of boys like a kung fu expert. I stood aside and watched as one boy went flying into the bus shelter with the flick of a hand. With the kick of a hoof, another boy was tossed into the middle of the square as if he weighed nothing, a third boy stared at the half-man, half-horse that was Joe with horror then took off as fast as his legs could carry him leaving only Trev and Bazza behind.

"Way to go Joe," I said in admiration from the wall as they cowered before him.

"You want to stay boys?" asked Joe looking down at them as a magnificent fork of lightning lit the sky followed by the deep boom of thunder.

Bazza took off after his friends leaving only Trev. He and Joe stood opposite each other sizing each other up like cowboys about to have a shoot out.

Suddenly Trev yelled, "Freak," and made a run for Joe. Joe chuckled, put his hand out and held him back by his forehead. Trev frantically punched the air in front of him but try as he might he couldn't get any closer. As his strength diminished, he began to look scared. He took one last look at Joe, turned on his heel and fled.

"You okay Danu?" asked Joe as Trev disappeared round a corner and out of sight.

"Uh yuh…" I nodded and this time I couldn't stop it. I fell to the ground in a proper faint.

When I came round a few moments later, I saw that Mrs Patel was running towards us through the rain. "I saw what was happening from the shop. I have phoned the police," she said. "They are on their way. Danu, are you all right?"

I looked around for Joe. He had returned to his usual form and was standing to my right looking at me with concern.

"You fainted," he said.

"Ma... wuh... buh... huh..." was all that I could stutter. "H...horse..."

"Horse?" asked Mrs Patel as she knelt down and put the palm of her hand on my forehead.

I pointed up at Joe. "Horse. Jupiter. Archer..."

Joe shrugged like he didn't know what I was talking about.

"I think she may be delirious," said Mrs Patel. "Maybe she was hit by lightning. We'd best get her home."

Joe nodded.

But I was sure that I wasn't delirious. Nor been hit by lightning. Nor had I imagined what I had seen. I'm not one prone to hallucinations. Not normally. Joe had transformed himself right in front of me and it had sure as heck blown a hole in my theory that he was an innocent eccentric who belonged to a club of similar nutters who liked to dress up and pretend that they were planets. Oh no. What I had witnessed a few moments ago was waaaaay out of the ordinary. He had looked like a god. He had fought with the strength of ten men. And a horse. *It couldn't be true could it?* I asked myself as I sat up. *It couldn't. Had Joe told the truth and he really was Jupiter? No. Not possible. It's crazy. Or is it?*

As the police sirens grew closer, I closed my eyes, sank back to the wet ground and allowed myself to be carried home.

Chapter Ten

Makeover madness

"When are they getting here?" asked Sushila who'd appeared on the doorstep first thing on Monday morning.

"Any minute," I replied. "Rosa and I are just having breakfast. Want some coffee or juice or something?"

Sushila nodded and stepped inside. I'd told her on the bus coming home from school all about the makeover people and she had asked if she could be here when they came as she loved watching makeover type programmes on the telly.

I felt so excited. Better than I had in ages. The flat makeover was the first thing I'd ever won in my whole life apart from a hamper of German sausages when I was ten and going through my vegetarian phase. My prize this time was going to be a lot more useful.

I led Sushila through to the kitchen where Rosa was making coffee and reading the stick-it notes that I'd left all over the kitchen for her. I introduced the girls then found a mug for Sushila.

"Kenyan or Columbian coffee?" I asked.

"Just coffee," said Sushila.

"And a biscuit? We have pecan or chocolate? And we also have cake. Home-baked by me," I said proudly.

Our kitchen was now stocked up like a normal kitchen because before she left, I had asked Aunt Esme if I could do an internet shop for food and stuff. She had been in such a hurry getting ready for her trip that she agreed and I'd had a great old time with her debit card. Think big, Joe had kept telling me so I had. I'd stocked the kitchen up with all sorts of goodies. Rosa had helped me and ordered the basics in like bread, cheese, pasta, vegetables, fruit and so on. We had found a great site that had pictures of the food as well as the prices so she would point to items and I'd click on them to go in our basket.

"What's going on?" asked Sushila when she saw the stick-it notes.

"I'm teaching Rosa English," I said. Last night we had decided that it would be a good idea after our slow attempts to communicate with the matchstick drawings. Instead of doing pictures, we were using words on stick-it notes and then sticking them on the appropriate object. Like DOOR on the door. JAM on the jam. Rosa was a quick learner and already could say most of the things in the kitchen.

As we fussed about making coffee, the doorbell went.

"Design man coming," said Rosa to Sushila who nodded back at her as we trooped out into the hall.

I opened the door to three peculiar-looking people. A severe-looking blonde girl in heavy black glasses and hair scraped back in a bun, a stocky man with a shaved head who looked like a builder and was carrying a big case, and a tall thin man with long wavy dark hair, a hooked nose and skin so pale that he looked ill. They were all dressed in head to toe black.

"You are Danu?" asked the thin man.

I nodded.

"I PJ. Zis is my team, Natalka and Oleksander. You may call zem Nat and Alex."

I must have looked confused because the team standing before me looked more like they worked in a funeral parlour than an interior design agency.

"*Ve're* your prize! Tadaaaah!" said PJ without a smile then he clapped his hands and ushered Nat and Alex inside. "Vy you iz staring at me?"

"Oh sorry," I said as I stepped aside so they could come in. I hadn't realized that I had been staring but there was something about PJ. Despite his nose and pale skin, he was incredibly handsome, like a romantic poet from another era. And he spoke with a foreign accent that I was trying to place. It sounded half Russian, half something else.

He tossed a long velvet scarf over his shoulder and swanned in, walking up and down the corridor looking at the walls, the skirting boards, the floors.

"So. Let's see vot ve 'ave here," he tutted as if he didn't like what he saw.

The name PJ rang a bell. "Hey. Do you know Joe Joeve?" I asked.

PJ turned and nodded. "Everee-*one* knows Joe. Ve call him ze godfazer. My studio iz on ze same street as 'iz café. Best kebabees in the area."

"And are you one of his planet club?"

"Planet club? Vot is this?"

"You know, Jupiter, Venus..." I didn't want to say too much in front of the others in case they thought I was mad plus I didn't know how much Alex and Nat knew about the possibility of their boss being a planet in his spare time. Since the episode with Joe in the square, I was more open to it being a reality. I'd decided, *why not?* No-one really knew who anyone was or where we came from or where we go or what we're even doing here on this planet so why shouldn't some people in human form be manifestations of the planets?

"*Oh oui*. Yeah, sure. *C'est vrai. C'est moi.*" He clapped his hands. "Some call me PJ, some call me Pluto. Pluto iz ze name, transformation iz ze game. So vere should ve start? Let's do ze tour!"

"Are you Russian?" I asked.

He flicked his hair back. "Russian, Ukrainian, Plutonese. Votever. I prefer to think of myself as Universal."

Yep, he's definitely one of them, I thought. *He talks in the same riddles. I wonder what he can do and if he's going to turn himself into anything peculiar like Joe did?*

But no. He was acting reasonably normally. He went from room to room up and down the corridor a few times hmming and tutting as Rosa, Sushila, his team and I followed.

"*Zut alors*," he said when he finally stopped.

"I know," I said as I caught up with him. "It's awful isn't it?"

"Hhmm. Not awful. Just empty. Each room it says, nozing."

"Nozing?" I asked.

"Nothing," said Sushila.

"Correct," said PJ. "Nozing. I have no idea who lives 'ere. Vot kind of person. Vot zey like. Vot zey don't like."

"That's what I said," said Sushila. "It's unlived in. Like a hotel."

"Exactly. A blonk canvas…"

"Blonk?" asked Suhsila.

PJ nodded. "Yes. Blonk, blonk…"

"Oh blank?" I asked.

PJ nodded. "Yes. A blonk canvas. Vich is marvellous. Vere shall ve begin? Alex. Nat. Take notes. Mizz Harvey Jones. Vot vould you like? You von ze prize, so ve do vot *you* vant. Any ideas?"

"Er…" I was suddenly seized by a momentary panic. What if we did a makeover and Aunt Esme didn't like it? I had no idea what her taste was really like. As long as everywhere was clean seemed to be the most important thing. "Um… Aunt Esme likes neat and tidy so maybe we should go for something simple, uncluttered."

"Ve could," said PJ. "But vot vould you like?"

He sat on the sofa and indicated that I should sit next to him. I perched next to him while his team stood behind like slaves guarding a pharaoh.

PJ snapped his long bony fingers. "Colours, samples," he said and Nat produced a pile of books from a huge bag and placed them on the table. "Okay, Danu and friends. Ve 'ave to make some choices."

We spent the next half-hour pouring through fabric samples, paint samples, catalogues of furniture, lights, floors.

"Do you vant traditional, modern, exotic, romantic? Vot you vant?"

I looked up from one of the books. "Um… something to make it look more homely. More like a place where people live, not just pass through. Somewhere you'd like to come back to."

PJ stared off into the distance as if visualising it in his mind. "Yes. I zink ve can do that. Yes. Leave it all viz me, Danu, ve're going to totally transform ze place!"

Oh dear, I thought. *I do hope that Aunt Esme will be happy with the result.* It was one thing acting the sulky teenager. Another redecorating her flat. Doubts were beginning to set in.

"Er, perhaps we ought to do just one room to start with… or maybe even one corner of a room? What do you think?"

PJ looked at me as if I had slapped him. "I zink zat zere are ozzers who vould have died to have zis prize. I zink zat zere are ozzers who appreciate who I am. And vot I can do." He clapped his hands and Nat and Alex stood to attention by his side. "Come on. Ve're leaving."

As I watched them go, I looked around at the cold empty room. If I let PJ go, I'd still be coming back to this night after night. Nothing would have changed. I remembered Joe's words, "think big". Dare I risk the wrath of Aunt Esme by going for the transformation or should I opt for not rocking the boat and leaving everything as it was? I ran after them.

"PJ, *PJ.* No. Please don't go. I'm sorry and I really do appreciate such a great prize. Please stay. Do what you have to."

PJ turned back from the front door and snorted. "Pfff! It's alvays ze same. People resist change more zan anything else." He put the back of his hand on his forehead and looked up at the ceiling with a pained expression. "If only zey knew." He looked back at me. "You 'ave to break down to break through you know. Can't make an omelette vizout breaking eggs."

"I know. Yes. Yes. Whatever, just don't go. I'm thinking big. I really am. I'm not resisting. Please make an omelette. Let's do this thing!"

PJ clapped again and this time, he almost smiled. "Excellent. Ve're going to have some great fun here."

Later that night when PJ had gone, I checked the astrology site to see if there were any other competitions or surprises to look out for.

There was just one word.

Mars.

Now what's that supposed to mean?, I asked myself as I got into bed. Mars is the name of a chocolate bar. One of my favourites in fact but what would that have to do with anything? Joe was intent on getting me to fatten up a bit. Maybe he was saying eat more chocolate? No problemo there. Or maybe he meant the planet Mars. It's one of the ten. I knew them all off by heart now. Sun. Moon. Mercury. Mars. Venus. Jupiter. Saturn. Uranus. Neptune. Pluto. And I'd been looking them all up in my astrology book. Jupiter was the planet of joy and expansion. Pluto the planet of death, rebirth and transformation. Venus of love, harmony and beauty. Now what was Mars again? I knew I'd read it somewhere... Mars... But before I had the answer I had drifted off to Zzzzzz...

Chapter Eleven
Red planet

PJ was true to his word. At six the next morning, he arrived with his team. Plus builders. And decorators. And carpenters.

By six thirty, the flat was a hive of activity with hammers banging and drills drilling. No way could I stay there with all the din so when Rosa left to go to one of her cleaning jobs, I left too with the intention of going into Osbury to see Joe and have a wander around the shops.

"I hope what PJ is doing is going to be all right," I said as we stood at the bus stop.

Rosa sighed, shrugged and, in the same way that I had when I was trying to tell her that my mum was dead, she acted out a gun being put to her head then someone trying to cut her throat.

"Exactly," I said. "Aunt Esme's going to kill me."

Rosa shrugged again then smiled. The bus came round the corner and we both got on. I glanced back up at the tower block and I swear I could see stuff being chucked out of the windows and floating down to the ground below. I closed my eyes quickly and prayed that they weren't throwing out any of Aunt Esme's prize items.

When I got to Osbury, I went straight to Joe's deli to get some breakfast and see if he had anything in store for me.

"Zodiac Girl reporting for duty," I said with a salute when I spied his jolly face behind the counter.

His face lit up to see me. "Danu. Sit. Eat."

A few minutes later, he had put a plate piled high with scrambled eggs, bacon, mushrooms and toast in front of me. I told him about PJ arriving and how he seemed to have taken over the flat and he nodded as if that was exactly what he expected.

"That's what Pluto does when it touches a chart," he said. "It is the planet of transformation. Of death and rebirth."

A fleeting feeling of panic went through me and I prayed that the death wasn't mine when Aunt Esme returned from her trip.

When I had finished breakfast, I intended to go and mooch around the shops. It was half term after all and I needed a break from my bad girl act at school. It had been very tiring. Joe however had other plans. As I ate the last mouthful, he handed me a piece of paper then checked his watch.

"You're just in time, the class starts in ten minutes," he pointed out of the window. "Out to the road, turn right and it's in the village hall."

"Class? But Joe, it's half term," I moaned but then I glanced down and read the leaflet.

Are you puny? Picked on?

Kicked around? Hair pulled? Bullied?

Had enough? I bet you have.

No need to suffer. You can put an end to it all

with Mario's Martial Arts.

I do kung fu. Tae Kwon Do. Hari Kari. Whack 'em back.

No experience necessary. All ages and sizes welcome.

Osbury Village Hall. Wednesday morning. 9.30am.

Be there. Or be pathetic.

"Hari *Kari?*" I asked. "Isn't that a way of killing yourself with your own sword Japanese style?"

"It is," said Joe with a chuckle. "Mario can be a tough taskmaster when someone irritates him. In the past, he used to overact to pupils who didn't pay attention but don't worry, he's mellowed slightly. I doubt he'll be forcing anyone to do Hari Kari here. What he will do though is teach you to look after yourself."

"But I have you Joe," I said. "You can do that 'turn yourself into a centaur' thing if I'm in trouble."

Joe put his finger up to his lips. "Shush. We don't want that getting out. I'm not really supposed to do that in public but those boys... well they annoyed me..."

"Remind me never to annoy you... or this guy Mario," I said. "Although it was pretty cool when those boys saw you..."

"It was, wasn't it?" beamed Joe. "Got rid of them all right. But I am only your guardian for a month. You have to learn to defend yourself."

I nodded. *Interesting*, I thought. He hadn't denied what I had seen the other night. So it wasn't my imagination after all.

"Why me, Joe?"

"Why what, Danu?"

"Why am I a Zodiac Girl?"

Joe looked at me with a gentle expression. "Same reason that you have the hair you do, the eyes you do, the personality you do and the experiences you do. It's in your chart. Usually being a Zodiac Girl happens at a turning point in someone's life. A make-or-break time. The planets conjoin to assist but after that it's what you make of it."

"I see," I said. I was certainly at a turning point in my life. No doubt about that.

Joe cleared my dishes away. "Go on then. Off you go."

I wasn't going to argue. Before he had come to my rescue the other night, I had felt scared despite my tough act. And the moment that the boys had pinned my arms back had replayed over and over in my mind when I'd tried to go to sleep later that night. What I should have done. Said. How I should have reacted. I knew I wasn't as fit as I used to be when I lived at home with Dad and played lots of sport at school. Plus I'd lost a lot of weight since moving in with Aunt Esme and her lettuce leaves. The one thing I did know though was that the experience the other night in the square with the boys wasn't one I wanted to repeat. Next time I wanted to be fit and fight back with confidence.

I got up and took up a kung fu stance. "Ah so, here I go," I said with an Eastern accent and karate chopped the air.

"Just asking to be Hari Kari-ed," laughed Joe. "Now get over there."

I made my way over to the village hall and when I got inside I saw that the class was already underway. A group of about ten people were sitting on mats while in front of them, one of the most striking men I had ever seen paced up and down. He was tall with skin the colour of dark chocolate and dressed in black tracksuit bottoms and a sleeveless T-shirt that revealed well-toned muscles on his arms.

I jumped as he yelled, "AGAIN", at someone on the mats.

"Yes sir!" a skinny young boy in the front row squeaked.

"YES SIR!" said the man as he put his face close to the young boys. "Let's have some ENERGY YOU MOUSE OF A MAN!"

The boy pulled back and looked like he was going to cry. "Yes sir," he squeaked again.

I closed the door quietly behind me and began to tiptoe in so as not to disturb the class. As I was attempting to creep towards the seated group, the man at the front stopped. Without even turning in my direction, he boomed, "WHAT time do you call this? You're LATE."

"Oh. Yes. Sorry. Er... I only just found out about the..."

He turned around. He really was remarkably good-looking, like a Hollywood movie star. Deep brown eyes, wonderful cheekbones and a chiselled jaw. He was almost too good-looking to be real and I felt myself blush as his gaze brushed over me.

"Rule number ONE. I like my students to be on TIME. Understood?"

"Yes SIR," chorused the gathered audience.

"You. Dreadlocks. Sit," he shouted at me like a

sergeant major.

Pff, I thought, *no need to be nasty. Just shows that looks aren't everything.*

"RUUUULE two. I like my students to be TIDY. We'll be working in close proximity. Noooooooooooo dreadlocks whipping about the place. You. What's your name?"

"Dee sir,"

"Deeser? What kind of name is that?"

"No sir. Dee sir. Short for Danu."

"So why did you say Deeser? Don't you know your own name?"

"I was being polite. Calling you sir, sir."

He hesitated for a moment before roaring, "CorRECT. Now sit and get rid of those dreadlocks before the next class."

You might be impressive to look at, I thought, *but I'm not going to take that from someone I've only just met who's not even a teacher at my school.*

"Why should I sir? They are clean."

"They don't suit you," he said. "You're a very pretty girl and you're doing yourself no favours."

"I... ah..." I was speechless. That wasn't the answer I'd expected. And part of me felt flattered that he'd said I was pretty.

"SIT!" the man suddenly boomed at me.

"Sit, sit," whispered a weedy-looking boy to my

right as he pulled on my hand. "If you get him mad, he takes it out on us in the exercises. Pleeeeeease."

The boy looked like he needed all the help he could get and I didn't want to make life difficult for him.

"Sorry sir," I said, saluted Mario and sat down.

"Sooo. As I was saying before we were so rudely interrupted. My name is Mario Ares. This is my class. I work you hard but I get results. No pain, no gain. By the time you all leave here, you will be experts in judo, Muay Thai, Ju-Jitsu, aikido, kendo…"

"Hari Kari," I called out before I could stop myself. Being cheeky in class had clearly become a habit.

Mario fixed me with a cold stare. "Okay. You. Stand. Approach."

"Now you're for it," said the skinny boy next to me. I strode up to the front.

"Okay, dreadlocks," he said when I reached the front. "Introduce yourself to the class."

I turned to face the assembled group which consisted of two very fat boys, three very skinny boys, two boys with bright red hair and very pale skin, two old ladies, one dressed in a pink track suit who was obviously besotted with Mario, the other who looked like she had broken her leg and an Indian girl who looked about Rosa's age.

"I… my name is Dee, short for Danu. Harvey Jones."

I went to sit down.

"And why are you here?" asked Mario.

"What – like on the planet or here in this village hall?"

"Don't you get clever with me young lady. I meant here in the village hall."

"To learn self-defence."

"SIR," bellowed Mario.

"SIR," I bellowed back.

"Now hit the deck," said Mario.

"Hit the deck?"

Mario pointed at the floor. "Give me twenty you girlie wuss."

"Girlie wuss?" I felt outraged. I wasn't girlie. And I wasn't a wuss. No-one was going to speak to me like that.

"Do them yourself," I replied. "And if anyone's the girlie wuss round here, it's you."

The group gasped in horror.

"Exactly what I thought when you walked in here," said Mario. "Brat. Spoilt brat. Bet you always get your own way, don't you?"

"What are you going to do if I don't do them? Give me lines to do? Expel me?"

Mario narrowed his eyes and fixed me with a cold stare again. I stared back. I was good at staring matches. I could make my eyes go out of focus and do it for ages. I had been champion at my last school. Plus I felt angry with Mario. Just who did he think he was? I had come to a self-defence class. Not to join the army. I turned to leave.

Mario dismissed me with a flick of his hand and turned his back on me. "Go on then. Run away little dreadlock princess. Have your own way. No time for timewasters here."

It was then that I read the logo on the back of his shirt: Red Planet Martial Arts.

Should have known, I thought. Red Planet. Mario was Mars.

Chapter Twelve

Worms

I felt close to tears when I got out of the class. I ran to a bench on the other side of the green away from the pavements that were now busy with morning shoppers. *What a horrid man*, I thought. He didn't know me at all or he wouldn't have said those things. Girlie wuss? Wuss? I wasn't. No way. I had been really brave when Dad had left. I hadn't cried at all after he'd hugged me goodbye then picked up his suitcase and gone out to the taxi that took him to the airport and the *other* side of the world. It was only later when I was in my room with Snowy and Blackie that I had let the tears flow. And even though I wanted to, I hadn't cried when I'd said goodbye to Mrs Wilkins when my taxi had arrived to take me to Aunt Esme's a couple of days later. I knew it would upset her too much if she saw me crying. And I hadn't cried when I said goodbye to Fran and Annie and Bernie and Jane. I knew they'd be upset too. They were all blubbing like proper girlie wusses when the car drove me away. But not me.

No, the only time I lost it was when I had to say goodbye to Blackie, Snowy and Spot. How was I to explain my disappearance to them? I could tell that they knew that something was going on because Snowy kept getting into my suitcase every time I tried to pack and Blackie would sit at the end of my bed looking at me with great sad eyes. On the morning that I left, I'd taken Spot an apple then gone and sat in the middle of the garden at the back of our old house with Snowy and Blackie on my lap for a last cuddle and then I'd howled like a baby. Mind you, so did Blackie and Snowy. We were a trio of howling howlers. But I'd been brave apart from that. I'd been brave the first time I'd found myself alone at Aunt Esme's with no company except for the telly and the dead pot plant on the balcony. I'd been brave when I started school and everyone was running around saying hi to their friends and not one person asked who I was or what I was doing there or tried to make me feel welcome at all. And I'd been brave when Trev and his horrible mates had tried to steal my phone. So girlie wuss? How DARE he? He had no idea what I had been through. And to call me a spoilt brat and a princess on top of all that. I hated him. And I hated Joe for having sent me to him. He was supposed to be my guardian and be looking after me, not introducing me to cruel insensitive meanies.

I got my astrology book out of my rucksack and looked up Mars.

To do with physical energy, stamina or goals, it said. Often depicted as the warrior. Well Mario fitted the bill perfectly.

From my bench, I watched people cruising up and down the street, stopping to gaze in windows, going in and out of the shops. Going into Europa for a takeaway sandwich. Going about their lives. Girls from my school. Some with their mates. Some with their mums. Suddenly I felt like I was going to cry. I didn't even have a mum to go shopping with, never mind a dad who didn't seem to care what I did.

Up above the sky was growing darker, threatening rain and I realized that I was cold. I only had a fleece on as the weather had been mild when I'd set out this morning. I got up to go home then realized that I couldn't. PJ was there doing the makeover.

Nowhere to go. No-one to talk to. The song that Joe had sung when I first met him ran through my head. "Nobody loves me, everybody hates me, think I'll go and eat worms. Big ones, small ones, fat ones, thin ones, see how the little one squirms."

At that moment, I spotted a worm wiggling its way along the ground. It looked so pathetic. And so small. I felt like picking it up and taking it home to look after. *Don't worry*, I said out loud. *I won't eat you.*

Then I thought, *God I am sad. Now I'm talking to worms!*

I sat on the bench a while longer and tried to decide what to do. I could call my mates back home on my normal mobile. But they'd probably all be out having a life. Hanging out and enjoying the half term. Speaking to them would only make me more homesick. As would talking to Mrs Wilkins. I didn't want to go back to the deli in case Joe asked how the martial arts class had gone and I couldn't bear any more criticism. I scanned the shops opposite. The magic shop? I could pop in and see Uri? No. He's too wacky. Not in the mood for him. Mars, Joe had said. He must have seen an encounter with Mario in my chart. Definitely not in the mood for him either, so no way am I going back to his class.

At that moment, my zodiac phone beeped that there was a message for me. I looked at the screen. "Transformation is a process. Before the butterfly comes the caterpillar and the cocoon."

Another of Joe's riddles, I thought as I got up and stomped some warmth into my cold feet. *Pff, well I hate riddles and I hate astrology, and I'm not going to let it or them control my life.*

Suddenly I had a brainwave. Okay, so maybe some of the planets were around in human form. Well I was going to pick and choose who I wanted to see, not the other way around. Pentangles. The hair and beauty salon. That was it. It was run by the beautiful blonde lady who had been in the deli on the day that I met Joe. Unlike Mario, she looked gentle. Joe had said she was Venus and at the time I'd thought he was barking mad. Well I knew better now. I found the page on Venus in my book. Planet of love, harmony and beauty, it said. *And about as opposite to Mars as you could get*, I thought. *Just what I needed.* Joe might say Mars. Well *I* say Venus. I would go in there and treat myself to a manicure or a facial or something. A bit of pampering in a warm environment. Heaven. Fran, Annie, Bernie, Jane and I use to play DIY beauty salons on Sundays when it was raining and there was nothing else to do and I'd always enjoyed our sessions. I had some spare money that Aunt Esme had left me and it would be an enjoyable way to keep out of the flat until the decorators left.

Feeling much happier now that I had decided to take back control of my life, I got up and made my way over to the salon.

A young girl with spiky red hair was behind reception when I opened the door and stepped inside.

"Er… is the lady with the blonde hair in today?" I asked.

"Nessa? Nah. She's gone down the suppliers with Trace," said the girl as she looked me up and down. "What do you want doing? Yer 'air? S'a bit of a mess innit?"

"No. I wanted a mani…" I caught sight of myself in the mirror. My hair *was* a bit of a mess. More than a bit. The front had gone all frizzy in the rain and my dreadlocks looked… dreadful, like straw-coloured cigars stuck to the side of my head. I looked like a mad girl. No wonder no-one wanted to be my friend. "Yes. My hair."

"Okay," said the girl. "Suppose I can do it for yer."

I glanced back at my reflection in the mirror and took a deep breath. "Yes. Okay. Thanks."

She led me to a chair, sat me down and tutted as she examined my hair. "Oh dear, oh dear, oh dear…"

"Can you just comb it out?"

The girl looked doubtful. "It could take hours."

"I have the time if you have."

"Sorry dahling but yer 'air's ruined. It's too far gone."

I looked at my reflection in the mirror. After months of being happy to look how I felt – the odd one out – suddenly I couldn't bear it a second longer. I wanted to look like me again. Dee. Normal.

The girl must have seen my look of disappointment.

"Look love, tell you what. I have an idea but you're going to have to trust me. I've just been on a course and learnt this fab new technique. You'd be perfect for trying it out on."

I glanced up at her. She looked sincere. I nodded,

closed my eyes and a few minutes later, all I could hear was the *snip snip snip* of scissors cutting hair.

"Sorted," said the girl a short while later.

I opened my eyes and shrieked. "OMIGOD! *Ohmigod*! Bat poo and a half! What have you done?"

If my appearance was strange before, it was even stranger now. I looked like I'd just joined the army and been given a number one cut. There was hardly any hair left on my head. "What's this supposed to be? The hedgehog look? I look like a bristle head. I thought you said you'd learnt a fab new technique?"

The girl looked offended. "I 'ave. And it looks betta than it did and..."

I got up from the chair and ran for the door.

"Oi. I 'aven't finished," the girl called as I ran out. "And you ain't paid…"

I didn't care. I looked awful. I ran for the bus and kept my head down until it drew up. Once on, I made a dash for the back and prayed that I didn't see anyone that I knew. I felt in shock. At least with the dreadlocks I looked like I had some style, some edge. Now I looked like I had just had the worst haircut ever. Which I had. My plan was to get back to the flat and hide in my bedroom for the next few years until my hair grew back.

Life cannot possibly get any worse, I thought miserably as I let myself into the front door half an hour later.

The flat looked like a bomb had hit it.

"Oh noooooooo," I wailed. "What happened?"

Floorboards were up revealing the joists underneath. Walls were stripped of paper, exposing the plaster and electric wires underneath. Units in the kitchen had been pulled off the wall leaving ugly gaps in the paint and it even looked like someone had attempted to knock down the wall between the kitchen and the living room.

"Holy crapoley. I'm a dead girl," I moaned as I surveyed the disaster that was left of Aunt Esme's flat.

PJ appeared out of the bathroom. "Oh you're back," he said cheerfully as he checked out my hair. "Hhhhm. Interesting haircut."

"I wish I could say the same for your decorating," I said as I slumped to what was left of the floor and surveyed the wreck. All the fight had gone out of me. I didn't care about anything anymore. My life was over.

Chapter Thirteen

Visitors

"Break down to break through," said PJ who didn't seem phased at all by my reaction. "Transformation is a process…"

"Before the butterfly, first the caterpillar and the cocoon," I finished for him. "Can't you guys come up with any original sayings of your own?"

PJ looked hurt. "But iz true and that *iz* my saying. Everyone's alvays using my sayings," he said with a pout. "Iz because I say such vise things about life and death all ze time…"

"Never mind that. The place is a mess. What am I going to tell Aunt Esme when she gets back?" I demanded as visions of Aunt Esme in full freak out played through my head.

"You von't need vords," said PJ who was clearly still feeling sulky. "The flat vill speak for itself."

"Oh yeah? And what's it going to say? Er… had a bit of a party while you were away. Sorry about the holes in the wall… and the ceilings…and the floors."

PJ flounced off. "You 'ave no faith. Just you vait and see. And if you're crossing ze room, be careful to walk on ze joists and *not* to stand on ze areas between ze joists as ze plaster isn't solid and you'll go straight down to ze floor below."

"I'm not stupid, PJ," I said as I tiptoed along one of the joists like a professional tightrope artist to see what they had done with my room. At least the floor in the hall and my bedroom was still intact although half of the ceiling had been taken down and someone had painted great daubs of different paint colours on the walls. When I caught sight of myself in the little mirror above the chest of drawers, I quickly turned it back to the wall then got onto my bed and snuggled under the duvet where I intended to stay until my hair grew back.

I must have nodded off because the next thing I knew was the sound of Rosa's voice.

"Dee, Dee, you is in there? Is time for eatings."

"Go away. I'm not hungry."

"Aunt says Dee must eat. Aunt phoned."

I stuck my head out. "Aunt Esme phoned?"

Rosa's expression on seeing me reminded me how bad my hair looked. I darted under the duvet again. "What did you say to her?" I asked from beneath the covers. "You didn't tell her about the flat makeover did you?"

"Best no I am thinking. Is great messingness out there. What is happening with the hair?"

"Oh disaster, Rosa," I said as I poked my head out. "You might as well see properly. Bad, bad haircut."

Rosa calmly surveyed what was left of my hair then her face broke into a smile. "Is better I am thinking. Can seeing the face more. You be pretty girl."

I sighed. "Except for the fact I look like a boy."

"Growing back it will," said Rosa. "Coming to eat. Kitchen is no more for cooking. I got pizza."

At the mention of food, my mouth began to water. "What about the flat destroyers? Have they gone?"

Rosa nodded as I got out of bed. "Back morning time," she said then she giggled. "More destroying then."

"I don't think there's much left to demolish," I said as I followed her into what was left of the flat to eat our supper amidst the chaos.

Later that night, I settled down in my bed and Rosa went off to Aunt Esme's room where she was staying in her absence.

Because I had slept so soundly earlier, I felt wide awake. As I tossed and turned, I became aware of the night sounds. The whistle of the wind in the windows. A train rattling past in the distance. A dog barking. Somewhere down below someone shouting. A car alarm going off. And then silence. Not even the sound of a clock ticking. Only my breathing. In. Out. In. Out. Then the sound of… what was it? Footsteps. On the stairs. Someone trying to be very quiet but not succeeding. *Probably the people upstairs had a late night,* I thought. But no. The steps had stopped. On our floor. I waited to hear a key in the lock and the sound of the door to the flat opposite open and shut as the lady who lived there went inside. But she was away too wasn't she? I seemed to remember Aunt Esme saying something to Rosa about it. And come to think of it, the footsteps hadn't sounded like hers either. She always wore high heels and they made a clickety click noise on the concrete stairs. These footsteps were more solid and they had sounded like a couple of people. Males. I strained to hear anything else. My heart began to pound as I heard a scraping sound in the hall outside. *At our door,* I thought as I sat bolt upright. *Omigod! Someone's trying to get in!*

I held my breath so that I could hear every minutia of sound. Yes. There it was again! A scraping fumbling sound. It would start and then stop. I decided to get up and go and see if Rosa had heard anything and was awake too. I got out of bed and tiptoed across the room. I opened the door as quietly as I could and crept into the hall. There was definitely someone outside. The scraping sound was louder in the hall, like someone was trying to pick the lock.

My heart was pounding like a drum as I crossed the hall. Who could it be? Maybe Aunt Esme back early from her trip. No. She had a key. Maybe whoever it was thought that the flat was empty. With all the activity of the day that was highly likely. People who lived round here were always telling stories of workmen having their tools and equipment stolen on unmanned sites. Empty flats broken into when occupiers were away. I heard the murmur of conversation outside so strained to listen. Whoever it was talking in whispers but I knew the voices. It didn't take me long to place them. It was that bully boy, Trev and his stupid friend, Bazza. Anger flooded through me. How *dare* they try to break into where I lived! I crept into Aunt Esme's room where I could see the dark shape of Rosa asleep in the bed.

"Rosa, Rosa," I whispered but she was dead to the world. Outside in the hall, the rustling noise continued. If one of them was picking the lock then they might succeed any minute and what would they find? A young woman who hardly speaks English and a puny-looking girl with a bad haircut. *Oh I wished I'd stayed in Mario's class and learnt some self-defence techniques,* I thought as my heart continued to pound in my chest and my mind began to fill with terrible images of what might happen. *Maybe this is why Joe sent me to the class. Maybe he's not so bad after all. He must have known we were going to be burgled and was trying to ensure that I could protect myself. Oh nuts. Why didn't I do as I was told?* I could just see the newspaper headlines: Teen with strange name and haircut murdered in her own bed by local assailants. She fought back but like a girlie wuss.

Oh God, what should I do? I asked myself. "Rosa," I whispered again and shook her ankles to wake her.

She woke with a start. "Wha…?"

"Shhh," I hushed her. "Someone's trying to get in the front door."

Rosa hid under the duvet. "Tell them go away. Go away now."

"But Rosa, you're the grown up. You tell them."

"I scary. No like dark either. Tell them go away."

I could see that Rosa wasn't going to be any good. It was up to me. I went into the hall. What to do? What to do? I didn't want to say anything in case they realized that it was me and that I couldn't fight back. *"Get something to hit them with,"* a voice in my head said. I tiptoed along to the living room to try and find a hammer or pickaxe. Unfortunately I forgot that the floor was up and there were only wooden joists across the room. I stepped onto an area between the beams and CRASH, my left leg went straight through the thin plaster.

"Ow*wow*!" I yelped before I could stop myself.

Behind me, Rosa had crept into the room. She was

carrying a torch and shone it in my face. "What you is doing?" she asked.

"Taking a bath. What does it look like I'm doing? I'm stuck. Oh God. Rosa hold on to me."

Between the two of us, I managed to free my leg and climb onto one on the joists then get back into the hall where the floor was still intact. I glanced back in the living room, light was streaming up from the floor below. I knelt down and looked through the gap to see the corridor downstairs.

Rosa began to giggle. "Good job not falling into downstair people's beddings. They be getting heart attack if someone falling in from ceiling."

Her shoulders began to shake with laughter.

"Shhhhh. Rosa. This isn't the time for jokes. In case you'd forgotten, some idiot is trying to break in."

"Yes. Me having idea. Turning on light and noise. They thinking many people here."

It wasn't a bad idea and I hadn't thought of anything better and I could still hear the sound of someone fiddling at the door. Luckily there were three locks as Aunt Esme was very security conscious and had made the flat as safe as she could.

"Okay, let's go for it," I said and turned on the hall light. Rosa ran back into Aunt Esme's room and reappeared with a radio which she turned on loud. Luckily it was a discussion programme, not music.

I crept back to the hall and put my ear to the door. The fiddling scrapey noise had stopped. I listened. Rosa turned the music up then called out loudly, "Jacob, hurry up in the bathing room?"

And then she replied to herself in a deep voice. "Be outing in a minute."

I gave her the thumbs up and listened at the door again. Finally, finally, I heard steps retreating.

"They gone?" asked Rosa.

I nodded and she came over to me and gave me a big hug. It was only then that I started shaking and Rosa had to put a blanket round me and make a mug of hot chocolate before it would stop.

We both slept in Aunt Esme's big bed that night but neither of us got much sleep.

Chapter Fourteen

Yes SIR!

"Oh you again," said Mario with a smug look when I got to his class the next day. I was first there and this time I was determined to stay no matter what insults he threw my way.

"Yes SIR," I said.

He checked me over to see if I was messing about but I stared him back eyeball to eyeball and didn't flinch once. I was dead serious and I think he got the message.

"Okay. You can start by taking your cap off," he said.

"I..." I was about to object as I had worn a black baseball cap to hide my hair disaster. I took it off. I didn't want him throwing me out for disobeying him.

He didn't even try to disguise his reaction. "Good God Almighty!" he gasped with horror. "What happened to your hair? Thinking about joining the army are you?"

"No SIR," I said. "Bad haircut SIR."

"You can say that again," he said.

"Bad haircut SIR!"

He gave me another penetrating look to see if I was messing but once again, I met his gaze. "Nessa will sort that out," he said. "Report to Pentangles one night after class."

"Yes SIR!" I said although I had no intention of going back in there. What could they possibly do to make it better apart from shave my head and fit me with a wig? No. I would wear baseball caps until it grew back.

The rest of the class began to filter in and take their places on the mats that Mario had set out around the floor of the hall. I glanced at them as they took their places. It was exactly the same group as yesterday.

"Right then you ugly bunch of losers," Mario started when everyone was seated. "This is the class that gives you the skills to get by. Will make you into prettier specimens. Now I want there to be an atmosphere of trust here so I'd like you all to get up and introduce yourselves to this creature here who has crawled in off the pavement." He checked my face to see my reaction to his insults but I just smiled back at him. *Call me what you like mate,* I thought. *This girl ain't budging.* "I know you did it yesterday," he continued, "but you're going to do it again. Why? Because I say so. Each of you, up, say your piece then back to your place as I don't want to spend all day on this." He motioned to a chubby blond boy to get up.

"Name?" asked Mario when the boy got to the front.

"Matthew."

"And you're here because?"

"Kids laugh at me at school. Call me fattie. Tubs. Had enough sir."

After Matthew was another fat boy. "Name, Cuthbert. Same as Matthew, had eeeeeenough SIR."

The old lady in the pink track suit got up next. "Nancy. Used to be a victim until I came to these classes. Poor me, little old lady. Not anymore thanks to Mario, I'm rough and I'm tough and no-one's gonna get me on a dark night and steal my handbag. No SIR!" And she did a couple of high karate-type kicks and split her trousers. "Oops! No matter. I've got another pair in my holdall." As she dashed off to change, I swear I saw Mario's face almost twitch with laughter but he soon recovered his stern expression.

The other old lady with the broken arm and bandaged leg got up. "My name's Lily and someone *did* get me on a dark night. Four of them there were. Nasty boys who smelt of cold chips and warm beer. Never again. Let me tell you all about it and my operations, ooooh I can tell you some stories, ooooh mi leg, mi arm, the pain, the pain, mi lumbago, awful it is…"

"Good for you, Lily," interrupted Mario. "You can fill everyone in more on your operations in the break. Today I'll be showing you how you can use that walking stick of yours as a weapon."

"Bring it on," said Lily as she held her stick aloft and shook it at an imaginary assailant.

The three skinny boys were next. Archie, Paul and Ian had similar stories. iPods nicked, mobiles phones stolen, teased at school, picked on for being puny.

"No worries lads, few more sessions here and the bullies will run a mile when they see you coming," said Mario as the boys beamed back at him. "Archie, I rename you Axeman, Ian, I rename you Iceman. Paul, I rename you… Paul the powerful. Now toughen up you big girls!"

Last up was the pretty Indian girl. "Usha's my name. Same story. Picked on for being a different colour. People call me Curry Head or tell me to get back to Thailand which is very insulting because my family are from Kerala in Southern India. I want to be able to walk down the street without feeling scared."

"You got it girl," said Mario then he jerked his chin at me. "Okay. So, good. Okay, now you, no-hair girl."

I got up and went to the front. "Last night someone tried to break into the flat where I live. I was really really frightened and although we scared them off, if it ever happens again I want to be able to defend myself. Also, not long ago, some kids tried to nick my phone and would have succeeded if a friend hadn't come by. I'm here to learn to fight back."

"Excellent," said Mario then clapped his hands. "Now on your feet you 'orrible lot! Let's get fit!"

Everyone got to their feet, even Lily who wobbled up with the help of Matthew and Cuthbert.

"Are you puny?" yelled Mario.

The assembled group shifted about on their feet and looked at the floor as if it held the answer.

"For heaven's sake, get some ENERGY up you lazy lot. 'HELL NO SIR' IS THE ANSWER. Now let me hear you."

"Hell no SIR," we attempted.

"AGAIN," roared Mario. "Are you losers?"

"HELL no SIR."

"A bunch of big girls?"

"HELL NO SIR," we roared back at him.

"Are you fighters?"

"HELL NO SIR," yelled Ian who wasn't thinking what he was saying, "I mean HELL YES SIR."

"HELL YES SIR," the rest of us joined in.

After exercising our lungs, Mario made us run round the hall, march on the spot, touch our toes and stretch our muscles.

"Okay, everybody," said Mario after we'd warmed up nicely, "up on your feet and let's see how you walk. Just relax and walk how you normally do."

We did as we were told and after a few laps of the hall, Mario clapped his hands. "Enough," he called. "Back to the mats."

Once again, we did as we were told.

"Paaaaathetic," said Mario as we sat before him. "Bunch of victims the lot of you, Nancy excluded. But no wonder the rest of you have been picked on. Matthew you waddle. Cuthbert you walk like a frail old man with knobbly knees. Ian, you've clearly spent too much time in front of your computer with those round shoulders. Stop slouching. Paul you mince along like you've got ants in your pants. Dee – head up, head high. Walk boldly. Archie, you look like you're begging someone to come and beat you. Oh poor me, poor little me. Anytime soon someone's going to get me. WELL NOT ANY LONGER. Up you get again. Get attitude in your head that says I am confident. I am in control. *DO NOT MESS WITH ME.*"

We stood up and glancing around, I could see what he meant. We did look like a puny lot waiting to be pounced on.

"What do I hear? I said WHAT DO I HEAR?" Mario growled.

"YES SIR," we shouted back at him.

"Okay," said Mario. "Now I want you all to imagine that attached to the top of your head is a helium balloon and attached to the bottom of your spine is a lead weight."

I did as he directed and felt myself grow two inches. It felt amazing. I glanced at the rest of the group and already I could see that we were all standing taller.

"Okay with that image in mind, go. GO. Walk. A one two three. NoOOOOO. Ian. Relax. All of you *relax*. Shoulders down. No slouching. Up straight. In charge." Leading the way, Mario began to walk around the room like he was leading us into battle. I really got into it. It felt good to be walking as if I owned the world not as if I had the weight of it on my shoulders.

The rest of the morning flew by. We did more warm-up exercises then went into learning some defence techniques. Mario showed us how to block anyone coming in for an attack by using our arms or our legs and in Lily's case, her stick. We learnt vulnerable points on the body and how to target them. How to use our elbows, feet, knees and hands by making a claw, using the heel or side of our hand, clenching it into a fist and using the knuckles. I never realized that I could do so many things with just my hands. It was totally brilliant. The heel of a hand to someone's nose could do some serious damage. And foot to groin even more, especially if the assailant was male! Matthew got a bit carried away with that move and kneed Cuthbert with too much force. Poor Cuthbert had to hobble off to the side to recover and for a while I didn't think he was going to rejoin the group. In the end he did and seemed relatively unharmed except for the fact that his voice had gone up a few octaves.

In the lunch break, I checked my zodiac phone. There was a text.

Jupiter meets Venus, it said.

I decided to call Joe to ask him what it meant.

"Hey Danu," he said when I got through. "How you doing? Meet Mario?"

"I did. I have, I mean, someone tried to break into the flat last night."

His voice sounded concerned. "You okay?"

"I am now but I was scared at the time…"

"It isn't in your chart that you get hurt," said Joe. "I would have warned you."

"I thought that's maybe why you had sent that message saying 'Mars' and sent me to Mario's classes?"

"Not exactly. All I could see was that there was an

encounter with Mars in your chart. How that manifests itself is up to you."

"I don't understand. You mean that it's not all predetermined?"

"Some of it is, some of it isn't."

"Joooooooe, don't do that talking in riddles again. What do you mean?"

"How you respond to events in your life, that's not determined. That's completely up to you."

"Ah… You mean like seeing a glass as half full or half empty depending on how you view it and what mood you're in?" I asked. Mrs Wilkins always used to say that back home.

"Sort of. It's back to swim or sink, the choice is yours. You can sulk and moan and be miserable about your situation or you can get up and do something about it. Which I know you are beginning to do. How's the flat coming along?"

"Looks like an earthquake hit the building. Maybe I'll say what you've just said to me when Aunt Esme gets back and sees her home ruined and starts frothing at the mouth. Oh Auntie, I will say, it's your choice, swim or sink, you can either see this as a disaster and moan about it or you can be glad and respond with joy. At which point she will clout me over the head and probably kill me. So yeah, thanks for those words of wisdom Joe."

Joe began laughing at the end of the phone. "I'm sure your aunt will be fine about it. In the meantime, enjoy the class with Mario."

"Enjoy! Hah. You wouldn't say that if you had seen what he's making us do this morning."

Joe laughed. "Ah but he's a great teacher."

At that moment Mario came to the door and called everyone to go back in. I noticed that he clocked my phone and raised an eyebrow.

"Quick Joe, your message," I said as I got up off the wall I'd been sitting on. "What did it mean Jupiter meets Venus?"

Joe just laughed. "You've got the book. You work it out."

"JOoooooooooe..." I objected.

"Danu," called Mario. "In here NOW."

It was no use. I could tell I wasn't going to get Joe talking and Mario looked in a mean mood. I clicked my phone shut and went back in.

"Okay, you snivelling bunch of wimps," said Mario as we all took our places ready for the afternoon session. "Who's going to be my next volunteer to be mashed up by the master?"

I raised my hand. "Me SIR!"

I hadn't had as much fun in ages.

On the zodiac site that evening, was a message from

Mario: There are only two types of people in this world. The quick and the dead. Winners and losers. Successes and failures.

That's six, I thought. *These planet people really can't count!* But I knew what he meant and I knew which one I wanted to be. The one who was alive without too many bruises!

Chapter Fifteen

Conga

The half term seemed to go by in the blink of an eye. Rosa and I fell into a routine of up early and out the flat, Rosa to her day job and me to the class with Mario. In the evening, to keep out of the decorators' way, Rosa would come and meet me at Joe's where we'd have supper and then we'd do a movie then home to bed. Sometimes Sushila would join us too. And a couple of evenings, her mates Amy, Chloe and Joele from school turned up with her. Seemed I wasn't the only one who wanted to get to know new people. In fact Joele and Amy said that they had wanted to get to know me better from day one but had been intimidated because I always seemed so aloof like I didn't need anything or anybody.

In the self-defence class, my skills improved daily and by the Friday afternoon, I could even throw Mario to the ground. At first I thought that he was letting me but he swore that he wasn't.

"I'm a good teacher," he said as he got up from the

mat where I had leg locked him down.

Regardless of whether he was letting me win or not, I felt a million squillion times more confident and walked out of his last lesson on Friday afternoon feeling like I could take on anyone.

Best of all though was that I discovered what "Jupiter meets Venus" meant. Or at least meant for me.

I was about to go into Joe's after the last class when who was coming out of the deli but Nessa. She took one look at me. "Zodiac Girl?" she asked.

I nodded and without another word, she had me by the collar and was dragging me off into her salon.

"Oh nooo," I pleaded. "Please. Not after last time."

"Trust me," she said and almost threw me into a chair by the hair washing basin. I could have arm locked her and tossed her to the ground but I decided not to resist. *Why not trust her*, I thought, *I haven't got anything to lose. At least not any hair anyway.*

I closed my eyes and let her do her work. She put on some space agey music and after all the physical exertion of the week, with the soothing touch of her hands as she washed my hair and the lavender scent of the shampoo, I soon drifted off. When I woke up and looked in the mirror later, I could hardly believe my eyes. A girl with shoulder-length glossy blonde hair stared back at me.

"Wha...?" I stuttered. "Is it a wig?"

Nessa tugged on the hair and I winced. No. It was definitely joined to my scalp. *Maybe she's a witch as well as a planet in human form*, I thought.

"Magic?" I asked.

"Sort of," Nessa grinned back. "Hairdresser's magic."

"But… how…?" I started.

Nessa showed me swatches of different-coloured hair that she had on a sample card by the mirror. "We can do anything these days. Good innit?"

"Really good," I nodded as I swished my new hair around like I was in a shampoo commercial. It was a vast improvement on my "sergeant in the army" crop and it felt great to look like the old Dee again.

Jupiter meets Venus. Jupiter is the planet of joy and expansion. Whatever it touches grows. Venus is the planet of love, harmony and beauty. The two meet and what do you get? Bingo. Hair extensions.

I laughed all the way to the bus stop.

Back at the flat an hour later, I opened the door expecting to see the usual dust and debris. Before I could step in PJ had pounced on me.

"Close your eyes, close your eyes," he said as he covered my face with the palm of his hand.

I quickly did as I was told and he led me down the corridor.

"Okay, looking now," he said. "Tadaaaah."

"Surprise," yelled a chorus of voices.

"Ohmigod," I gasped as I opened my eyes to see Mr and Mrs Patel, Joe and Rosa, Uri, Mario, Nessa, *(how did she get here so fast?* I wondered*)* Nat and Alex, Sushila, Joele, Chloe and Amy all standing there in front of me with big grins on their faces.

"Wha…?" I blustered.

Rosa came over to me and put her arm round me. "Look. Looking around you," she said.

If I had been shocked at the transformation of my hair, it was nothing in comparison with the change in the living room. It looked fabulous. The walls had been painted a soft honey colour and there were light gold muslin curtains at the window. The old faded carpet had gone and in its place was a polished light oak floor. The book shelves had been filled with books which on first glance were a mixture of fiction and travel. My favourites. In the fireplace, the empty vase at last had flowers in it – large stems of yellow roses. A two seater honey-coloured sofa had been added adjacent to Aunt Esme's cream Italian sofa which had finally had its wrapping taken off it and been strewn with the most plush cushions in the same colour as the smaller sofa. The whole effect was warm and stylish.

"There's more," said PJ as he took my hand and led me into the kitchen. That too had been transformed. He had left the units where they were but put new light oak doors with silver handles on so giving the room a modern feel. The walls had been painted bright yellow with shiny green and gold tiles on the splash back areas giving the room a cheerful bright look. Best of all though was when Rosa came in and opened cupboards and drawers to show that they had all been stocked with utensils, cutlery, pots, pans, plates, cups, saucers, basic food and in one gleaming storage tin on one of the surfaces were biscuits, cakes and chocolates.

As Rosa supplied our guests with drinks and nibbles from our newly furbished kitchen, PJ showed me around the rest of the flat.

In the bathroom, he had gone for minimal and modern. It was all white tiles, white walls and a whole wall of mirror which made the room look twice the size that it was.

"As it iz such a small space, I took out zat old bath and put in a power shower," said PJ. "You are liking?"

"Fab," I said as I looked around. No detail had been left out. A silver towel rail, a shelving unit housing big white fluffy towels, a shelf full of fab-looking scented bath lotions, potions and soaps to try out, and a dab of colour with a bunch of purple freesias in a small vase on the window ledge above the sink. "Fab, fab and fabber."

I grinned at PJ as he led me down to look at the

bedrooms. Rosa had been sleeping on the floor in my room for the last few nights while they worked in Aunt Esme's room. I felt full of trepidation as I opened the door as this was the room that it was most important they got right. I needn't have worried. PJ had worked his magic in there too and picked a soft lavender colour for the walls and sky blue for the blinds. The effect was simple, cool and clean, a reflection of how Aunt Esme liked to dress. I was sure that she was going to love it.

"And lastly your room," said PJ.

As we crossed the corridor to my room, I thought that he couldn't have done much as he'd only had one day in there because Rosa and I had been sleeping in there. Once again, I was wrong about PJ. In my tiny room, he'd managed to create more space by putting in a high bed that you climb up to with a ladder. It meant there was a whole area of space underneath. In there was a desk with my computer, a chair and bookshelf. On the wall opposite the bed were posters of all the places I wanted to visit some day: India, Africa, Europe, South America. The Moon. Jupiter. And on the bookshelf next to the desk, photos in bright coloured frames. There was one of Spot, Snowy and Blackie. One of Fran, Annie, Bernie and Jane. One of my dad and one of Mrs Wilkins.

"Rosa showed me your photos," said PJ. "I hope you

von't mind but I vanted to put zem vere you can see zem every day to remind you zat you're not alone."

"No, I don't mind at all. PJ, thank you so much…" I felt lost for anything else to say and was relieved when Uri appeared at the door with a carrier bag.

PJ gave me a low bow. "You iz most velcome. Iz your birthday. Iz good present no?"

I felt a lump in my throat. "I thought everyone had forgotten," I said.

"Forgotten? You iz Zodiac girl. How we forget? No. No vay. Now. Iz party time," he said and produced a box full of silly party hats, poppers and blowers. When we joined the others back in the living room, we soon had the hats on and when Nessa suggested that we do a conga around the flat, it seemed the perfect thing to do. We lined up and with Joe in the lead wearing a Napoleon type hat and a patch over his eye. We put our hands on the person in front's waist and set off.

"Ta dah dah dah dah dah da-aaa, ta dah dah dah dah daaaaaaaaaaaa," we sang at the top of our voices and kicked our legs out to the right and then to the left as we danced down the hall, back around the living room then back into the hall – just in time to see Aunt Esme come through the front door with her suitcase.

She didn't look amused.

Chapter Sixteen

Freaky deaky

I tried to explain. I really did.

"Mr and Mrs Patel and Rosa you already know," I said after she'd chucked everyone out and had properly taken in the makeover, "Sushila, Amy, Joele and Chloe are from school and I'd have thought that you'd be *glad* that I'm making friends."

"And the others?" asked Aunt Esme.

"The others? Yes... well that's what so totally amazing and I know it might sound a bit strange, I myself found it a bit weird in the beginning, but they are... er...um... planets..."

"Planets?"

I nodded. "Yes. Planets who have manifested in human form and live locally."

Aunt Esme didn't look impressed.

"And what's more brilliant, they're all my personal friends."

She gave me a look of great disappointment and began to walk towards her bedroom.

"Honestly," I said as I trooped after her. "Nessa is Venus and she runs the beauty salon. Uri is Uranus. He runs the magic shop and the internet café. Mario is Mars and teaches self-defence. He's really cool when you get to know him. And Joe, he's my favourite. He's my personal guardian for a month seeing as I'm Zodiac Girl. He's Jupiter and he runs the deli."

Aunt Esme had looked at me in despair. "Zodiac Girl? Mars? Venus? What are you talking about? That chubby man is Jupiter!? You'll be telling me that Neptune owns the bakery next."

I burst out laughing. "No. He runs the chippie. It's called Poseidon. You know, Poseidon, Neptune, king of the sea. I looked it all up in my astrology book."

Aunt Esme gave me another long-suffering look. "In that case the Moon would run the cheese shop then?"

"As if! No. She'd be hopeless at that. The Moon is Miss Luna. She works as a counsellor at our school and between you and me *is* a bit loonie petunie. Of course there are a few others I haven't met. I saw Hermie once in the deli, he's... what is it? Oh yeah – the manifestation of Mercury and works as a motorbike messenger boy and he's very, very handsome. Saturn is a headmaster somewhere..."

While I'd been talking Aunt Esme's expression

went through a kaleidoscope of emotions: disappointment, disbelief, outrage and concern. In the end, she put her hands up. "Enough! Enough Danu. Of *all* the things you've done to try to upset me, this has to be the most insane."

"But Aunt Esme, this is true. It really *really* is."

"Enough Danu. I won't hear another word. Now go to your room."

"But… but… you haven't even said what you think of the makeover yet. Your room. The sitting room. Isn't it all fabulous? Don't you love it?"

Aunt Esme looked around her and her mouth did that shrinking thing it does when she's angry. "Love it? *Love* it? Danu I don't know how this all happened but how am I supposed to pay for it?"

"But Auntie, it's free. See, I haven't told you about PJ yet. He's Pluto which is the planet of transformation. I won him in a competition… at least not him but a makeover for the flat done by him. He works as an interior designer. So nothing to worry about. Don't you love it?"

Aunt Esme pointed at the door. "Danu. Go to your room while I think about this and what to do next. *Now!*"

I did as I was told and spent the time in my new work area emailing my old mates. I had been rubbish about keeping in touch with them while PJ and his team had been in the flat and there were loads of emails from them all asking where I'd disappeared to and not to forget them. As I set about replying to them, part of me felt annoyed with Aunt Esme. Not a word of gratitude and she hadn't even bothered to come and look at my room.

After ten minutes, I heard a knock.

"Danu, I'm popping out for five minutes to get some cigarettes."

"But you don't smoke."

"I do now. I've just decided. And I might start drinking as well."

I heard the front door open and close and went back to my emails.

As I was writing, a pop-up flashed up on the left-hand corner of my screen. It was from Joe. "Quick, follow your aunt," it said. "She needs you."

Hah! Just shows how little he knows Aunt Esme, I thought. *She doesn't need anybody*. Then I remembered what Joele had said about me and how I looked like *I* didn't need anyone or anything. Could Aunt Esme possibly be the same? Hiding behind her tough exterior.

I got up and went through the flat to the window in the kitchen which looked out over the square. It was wet, dark and windy out but there didn't seem to be anyone around. I saw Aunt Esme come out of

Mr Patel's corner shop and begin to cross the square. She seemed okay. Maybe Joe meant she needed me to be more patient with her or something.

I was about to turn back and return to my room when a movement on the opposite side of the square caught my eye. I strained to see. Someone was over by the alleyway that led away from the square. My heart skipped a beat when I realized who it was. *Oh nooooooooo*. It was the terrible twosome, Trev and Bazza and they were creeping up on Aunt Esme.

I raced to my room and dialled Joe on my zodiac phone.

"Danu. You got my message?" he asked.

"Yes and you were right," I said as I headed out of the flat and took the stairs two at a time. "Aunt Esme's in trouble. Those boys who tried to steal my phone are after her."

"How many?" asked Joe.

"Two I think but the others may be there too so hurry," I urged as I reached the ground floor at full pelt. "Can you come and do that centaur thing?"

"You can take them," said Joe and hung up.

"Joooooooooooe…"

Too late. He'd gone and the boys were almost upon Aunt Esme who was walking ahead of them totally oblivious. I shoved my phone into my pocket and burst out of the double doors to our block just in time to witness them grab her from behind.

She shrieked and dropped her bag.

"Leeeeeeeeeave her ALONE!" I yelled.

When Aunt Esme saw me, she looked even more horrified. "Danu, go back. Get back inside."

Trev turned and saw me heading towards them. He immediately began to sneer. "Well if it ain't little miss dreadlocks with the posh phone," he said and quickly checked around the square. "Lost your locks have you?"

"None of your business," I replied as I came to a halt.

"So where's your fat friend tonight eh?" Trev jeered. "The freaky one with a backside like a horse's."

"He's coming," I said. "And if he doesn't, one of his friends will."

"Danu, please *run*!" pleaded Aunt Esme as she unsuccessfully tried to wriggle away from Bazza's grip.

Joe's words echoed in my head. "You can take them."

I took a deep breath and remembered Mario's words on the last day of his class. "Don't ever let them see if you are frightened. Explode and move."

I took another deep breath. "HIYAAAAAAAAH," I screamed as I leapt towards Trev, put my foot outside and behind his leg, my palm up to his chin, pushed with all the force I could muster and over he went. "Elbow Aunt Esme," I called as I ran and wrestled Bazza from behind to let go of her. "Use your elbows."

Aunt Esme did exactly as she was told and delivered a few swift back jerks. I went for his eyes and he quickly released her.

By this time, Trev had recovered and was struggling back to his feet. I didn't give him time to recover and ran towards him, stepped between his legs and kneed him neatly in the groin. "I hope you have an excellent career as a soprano," I said as once again he toppled to the floor.

On seeing Trev writhing in pain, Bazza looked uncertain but soon regained his composure. "No-one knees my mate," he growled as he ran towards me. But I was ready. I ran towards him with my arms raised and he was so busy trying to work out if I was going to punch him that he didn't notice that I'd put my right foot out and over he went, landing on a heap on top of Trev.

"Come on," I yelled to Aunt Esme who suddenly seemed to have frozen to the spot. "Run."

I grabbed her hand and raced towards the apartment block and up the stairs. We flew into the flat, quickly put the chain across the door and double-locked the locks. Behind us, I could hear the sound of police sirens while at the same time, my phone rang in my pocket.

Aunt Esme slumped to the floor as I answered the phone.

"You okay?" asked Joe's voice.

As I was talking I ran to the kitchen window to see if the boys were going to try and follow us. No chance. Down below was the wonderful sight of them being handcuffed and carted off into the back of the police van.

"Joe, why didn't you come?" I asked breathlessly.

"I called the cops instead," he said. "In case you needed back-up. Sometimes you've got to make use of the facilities here on Planet Earth. Did they get them?"

"They got them," I said. "Thanks." Behind me in the hall, I could hear the sound of Aunt Esme sobbing. "Better go Joe. Aunt Esme needs me."

"Told you she did," he said then hung up.

I went back into the hall and sank down next to Aunt Esme. "Hey, it's all right now. The police have got them."

I put my arm around her but that only made her cry louder.

"Aunt Esme, what is it? We're safe now. What can I do?"

"N...n... nothing..." she sniffed.

"Well I can't leave you here on the floor. Come on, get up. Come into the sitting room."

She did as she was told and snuffled after me with the meekness of a little girl who had had a nightmare. I let her cry a little then she finally wiped her eyes and looked around the room. That set her off again.

"Uhuh… uhuh… *waaaaah…*"

"Oh God," I said as I looked around. "You hate it don't you? I'm sorry. I… I… suppose I should have waited…"

"No. No… (*sniff*) uhuh… (bigger *sniff*) I… I… l… l… love it. I *love* it. I love *all* of it."

"So why are you crying?"

"Because I'm so useless and have been rubbish at looking after you and you've been unhappy and it's my fault and it's no wonder you want to leave and no wonder no-one ever comes here and I don't have any friends and have to work all the time to pretend that I have a life when really I don't," Aunt Esme blurted without stopping for breath, "and I'm lonely and so glad that you're here so that I don't have to come back to an empty flat any more. All I ever wanted was a real home but I am totally useless at it even the pot plant I bought died because nobody or nothing wants to stay around me for long… uhuh… buhuh… *waaaahhhh…*"

While she sat and cried like a baby, I scanned my mind what to do. Phone my dad? Phone Joe? Make her a cup of tea? In the end, I just held her hand and let her cry it out.

And then she began to laugh. And that was even more freaky deaky. I began to think that maybe she was cracking up altogether and I ought to call someone and get her carried off and locked up.

And then she hugged me.

"Danu. Do you think we could maybe start again. Me and you?"

Epilogue

Aunt Esme and I moved home three months later.

It was a shame to leave our new posh flat but we had outgrown the place and needed somewhere bigger – not only for entertaining the constant stream of visitors that always seemed to be round lately but also so that Rosa could have a room with us. When Aunt Esme realized that Rosa had been sleeping on the sofa at her cousin's house, she invited her to come and live with us straight away.

The most perfect cottage came on the market only half a mile away from Osbury and Aunt Esme leapt at the chance to own it and put in an offer. At first we thought it was going to be too expensive but thanks to PJ's marvellous makeover on the flat, we made a profit on the sale which helped pay for the cottage. Of course, we hired PJ's services straight away and he made the cottage look wonderful. It has four bedrooms, one for me, one for Aunt Esme, one for Rosa and one for Dad or my brother should they ever come to visit.

Best of all it has a garden out back with apples trees and a vegetable patch. My brother Luke has already been to stay a few times. I think he has a crush on Rosa which is why we're seeing more of him. It's nice to see him whatever his excuse for being here. Joe and Mario are also regular visitors and although my month as Zodiac Girl is over, I still go to Mario's classes and Joe still passes on his favourite recipes. Rosa, Aunt Esme and I have all become tip-top cooks. My astrology book says that everything Jupiter touches expands. And that has certainly been true, including our waistlines!

Aunt Esme cut back on her hours at the office and is altogether more relaxed and happy these days. We've become good friends in fact. She still hasn't accepted the idea about the planets being here in human form and I haven't pushed it with her. One thing at a time and she does like Joe and Mario and that's what is most important.

Best of all, we have a dog and a cat. Aunt Esme and I went to the animal rescue centre together and chose them. The dog is a red setter with gorgeous copper-coloured hair. We called him Bluey. The cat is a black Persian with vivid orange eyes. We called her Honey. Like Aunt Esme and I, I think both of them are glad to have a home and space to run around after being cooped up in a cage.

At school, things couldn't be better. Nit Nurse is extremely happy that I no longer have dreadlocks nor hair extensions as my hair grows quickly and I don't need them any more. Joele, Chloe and Sushila have adopted me as part of their group and although I will never forget my friends back home, it does feel great to have mates to hang out with who live nearby and go to the same school as me. My grades are back up again and next term we're going on a school trip to Italy. I am going to write it up as the first of my "travel diaries".

Dad will be back at Christmas. Now that I have a proper home, I don't mind so much that he's away, in fact I think it will be nice for him to come back to somewhere welcoming and cosy.

And as for Trev and Bazza, the police picked them up on the night that they tried to attack Aunt Esme. According to the local paper, the police found a whole pile of stolen goods from recent break-ins at Trev's and now both of them are doing time.

Part of me feels sorry for them. They didn't need to have acted so stupid but then they didn't have the planet fabsters to help them like I did when I was acting like a dingbat. At the beginning of term, it felt like my life was over but now, it feels like it's just begun. I feel more like my old self. The real Danu.

Unafraid of the world and happy with my life. I was so unhappy when I was angry with everyone and everything.

At the end of term, when Mr Beecham asked me to stand up in class and read my latest poem, this is how it went,

> "My aunt is full of chocolate cake,
> My guardian is a star,
> The planets, they look over us
> And home is not that far."

The Sagittarius Files

Characteristics, Facts and Fun.

November 22 – December 21

One of life's positive people – that's Sagittarius in a nutshell. They see the best in others and they are always thoughtful and generous. They are good at seeing both sides of an argument... empathy could be their middle name. Their optimistic attitude is contagious.

However, being a fire sign means they can be impatient and even self-destructive if things don't work out how they want them to. They can be oversensitive sometimes... chilling out a little now and again would help matters.

Element:	Fire
Colour:	Blue, Purple, White
Birthstone:	Lapis Lazuli
Animal:	Horse, Dog
Lucky day:	Thursday
Planet:	ruled by Jupiter

Sagittarius best friends are likely to be:
Gemini
Aries
Leo
Sagittarius

Sagittarius enemies are likely to be:
Scorpio
Pisces

A Sagittarian's idea of heaven would be:
going roaming on safari

A Sagittarius would go mad if:
someone kept proving them wrong all the
time... it's their way or the highway!

Famous Sagittarians:
Katie Holmes
Brad Pitt
Britney Spears

Here's the first chapter of another brilliant Zodiac Girls story, Discount Diva.

Chapter One

The Crazy Maisies

I wish, I wish, I wish I could go, I thought when our form teacher Mrs Creighton first made the announcement.

"… I will be taking names from all you Year Eight girls in the next week," she continued. "All those who want to go must register before the end of May which only gives you a week."

A school trip to Venice. Four days in sunny Italy. I wanted to go more than anything, ever, since the beginning of eternity and even before that.

"You going to put your name down, Tori?" asked Georgie when the bell went and we headed out of the classroom for the lunch break.

I shrugged my shoulder as if I didn't really care. "Maybe," I said.

"I definitely am," said Megan catching us up and linking arms. "Mum said I could go on the next school trip wherever it was."

"Me too," said Hannah linking arms with Megan.

"Me too," said Georgie. "Which means you have to come Tori. It wouldn't be the same without you. The Crazy Maisies hit Europe."

Me, Hannah, Megan and Georgie. We called ourselves the Crazy Maisies. My mum used to call me Crazy Maisy when I was little and acting daft. Me and my mates act daft a lot, hence the name.

"Venice isn't *that* great," I said. "Too many tourists. Florence is much more interesting." Hah. Like I'd been to either of them. Not. But I had heard my well travelled Aunt Phoebe saying that Venice was so full of tourists these days that you could hardly move.

"You *have* to come," said Hannah. "And so what if there are loads of tourists? We'll be four of them!"

"Yeah," said Georgie. "Italy here we come."

I felt a sinking feeling in my stomach. I was so going to miss out but I could never tell them the real reason why I couldn't go.

"Si signora, pasta, cappuccino, tiramisu," I said trying to remember all the Italianish words I had ever heard and to distract them from trying to persuade me to go. I'd have to think up some excuse that they'd all buy later.

"Linguine, Botticelli, Spaghetti…" Megan joined in.

"Da Vinci, Madonna, pizzeria, Roma," said Hannah.

Then they started singing a song that we'd done in music class last term. We'd had a supply teacher who had us singing songs from around the globe. "Trying to broaden your horizons," he said as he taught us folk songs from Italy to Idaho. By the end of term however, I think he was glad to broaden his horizons and move onto another school where the pupils weren't tone deaf.

"When the moon hits your eye like a great pizza pie, it's amore…" my mates chorused off key and in terrible Italian accents.

A few girls from Year Nine sloped past and looked at us as if we were bonkers. I play acted that I wasn't with them but Georgie dragged me back and Hannah and Megan got down on their knees, put their hands on their hearts and continued hollering away at the top of their voices.

Mad. They all are. And they'll have a great time in Venice that's for sure. Another thing was for sure: no way would I be going with them. Not a hope in hell.

In the break, we went out into the playground, found a bench on the sunny side and did each other's hair. When we first met, only Georgie, out of the four of us, had long hair. After a short time hanging out together, we all decided to grow it to the same length so that we could play hairdressers and long hair is best for experimenting with. Georgie and Meg are blonde although Megan's hair is thicker and golden blonde whereas Georgie's is fine white blonde. Hannah and I have standard brown hair although Hannah has had chestnut highlights put in hers lately. It looks totally cool. I'd love to have highlights but that's another thing to add to the "not going to happen unless my mum wins the lottery" list. I think Georgie's the prettiest of the four of us although Megan and Hannah are good looking in their own ways too. Hannah could pass for being Spanish. She has olive skin and amazing dark brown eyes which look enormous when she puts make up on. Megan has a sweet face, cornflower blue eyes and a tiny nose like a doll. Out of all of us, boys mostly pay attention to Georgie and me though. Hannah and Megan say it's because I am pretty too but sometimes I wonder if the main reason that boys talk to me to get in with Georgie. I'm not huge on confidence in that department. Although somedays I can look okay, I could look heaps better if I got my hair done properly and bought some fab new clothes and make up, but I doubt if that's going to happen any time soon. Reason being, my family are broke and a half, so it's hard trying to keep up on the appearance front. Most of my clothes come from second-hand shops but I worry that my mates will find out. At school, girls who don't wear the latest designer gear get called Nickynonames because their clothes don't have recognisable labels. Megan, Georgie and Hannah have no idea that I'm Queen Nickynonames.

"I think we should go for a really sophisticated look when we're in Venice," said Megan as she pulled back Georgie's hair and began to braid it.

"No. I think we should wear it loose," said Hannah.

"Yeah," said Georgie. "Loose and romantic looking. There might be some cute Italian boys to flirt with."

Oh no! Boys! Italian boys. I hadn't thought of that. What if one of my mates got a boyfriend and I wasn't there to share it all with them? What if all *three* of them got boyfriends and had their first kiss? It might happen. I've heard that Italy is a really romantic place. Romeo and Juliet happened over there and they were way loved up. I've also heard that Italian boys are very hot blooded. (I'm not totally sure what that means and whether they really do have hotter blood than us on account of living in a hot climate. Whatever.) Apparently they are more forward than English boys who mostly seem more interested in computers than they do in girls.

Anyway, I would be left so far behind in the game of lurve. I'd be like Cinderella left at home while everyone else went to the ball. Erk! That would be freaking *tragic*. The Crazy Maisies did everything new together, that way we could talk about it all and see how we all felt.

"Ow," said Hannah with a wince as I brushed her hair up into a pony tail. "You're hurting."

"Sorry," I said and made myself brush more gently. I didn't mean to take my frustration out on her but all the talk for the next few weeks would be about the trip. And then they'd go and I'd be on my own. And then they'd come back and all the talk would be about the trip again. And I'd have nothing to say because I wouldn't have been there. I'd be left out. It would be awful. Luckily Megan changed the subject and began making plans for the weekend. A new comedy movie was on at the local complex. Of course, everyone was up for seeing it.

"Brill!" said Georgie. "And we could go for snacks afterwards?"

Megan and Hannah nodded enthusiastically. "Loads of those Mexican spicy cheesy taco thingees. I luuuurve them."

"Ice cream for me," said Georgie. "Pistachio with… strawberry."

"Pecan fudge is my fave," I joined in.

"We'll have to do the early show, about six o'clock or Mum won't be able to pick me up," said Hannah.

I did a quick calculation as they were discussing how they were going to get there and back and what they were going to eat. I'd need money for the movie. Bus fare. Snack. Coke... Nope. No way I could do it on my pocket money. I get about a quarter of what my mates get and some weeks when things are really tight, Mum can't give us anything at all – us being me, my elder sister Andrea and two brothers William and Daniel. I took a deep breath and got ready to apply my usual philosophy: *when the going gets tough, the tough bluff it.*

"I can't make it tonight. Mum got me and Dan and Will tickets for the Cyber Queens gig."

"The Cyber Queens? Wow! You *lucky* thing!" said Georgie.

"You've kept quiet about that this week," said Megan. "Those tickets are like the hottest in town."

Hannah playfully punched my arm. "Yeah. Why didn't you tell us?"

"Mum only told us last night. It was a surprise for when we got home."

"A surprise? That's *so* mint," said Georgie. "She's so cool your mum. I wish my mum did stuff like that. I bet my mum hasn't even heard of the Cyber Queens. Can she get the rest of us tickets?"

"Don't think so," I replied. "I think she got the last ones."

"Take your digi camera," said Hannah, "Take lots of pics to show us."

"Sure," I said.

I felt guilty when the bell went for afternoon lessons. Not only did I not have tickets for the Cyber Queens but I don't have a digi camera either even though I'd told everyone that my gran had got me one as an early birthday pressie. I lied. I don't really like doing it but sometimes it's necessary. I have to make things up so that they don't think that I'm a total loser. My mates all have rich parents who buy them all the latest gear: iPods, mobiles phones with cameras, computer games, designer gear and they've all got their own telly and their own computers in their bedrooms. I don't have my own bedroom. Not even my own bed. Not really. I have to share a room and a bunk bed with my sister, Andrea. Sometimes I sleep on the downstairs sofa just to get a bit of space, though even then I have to share it – with our cats, Marmite and Meatloaf (My brother Will named them. Marmite's black and Meatloaf is tabby.) Anyway, my mates would surely dump me if they knew the truth about my situation and how poor we really are compared to them.

When we first all started hanging out together as

a group at the beginning of this year, to put them off coming round, I told them that our house was being decorated from top to bottom, kitchen, bathroom, the lot. I keep telling the girls that we're having "nightmares" with the builders who keep letting us down. It's an expression I've heard their parents use a million times. So far, they haven't been round a lot but when they have, my excuses have worked because the fact is, our house does look like it's in the middle of being decorated. The walls are patchy with daubs of paint here and there where one of us decided to try out some paint samples but there wasn't enough dosh to buy the paint. There are no carpets on the stairs. The carpets that are down on the floor are worn. There are floorboards up here and there. The whole place looks like it needs ripping out and redoing from top to toe so my story has never met with any questions. Sometimes I think that Georgia may have twigged but she's never come out and said anything, not yet anyway. It can be stressful on the rare occasions when the girls do come over though as I'm afraid that Andrea, Will or Dan might blow my cover. Instead, I try and make sure that we hang out at Megan, Hannah or Georgie's houses. I say, oh the floor's up again or the scaffolding is a bit dodgy or the water's off or something. They're so sympathetic that I feel rotten sometimes especially as

Georgie seems to like coming to our house and she always brings something with her like some fab shortbread or expensive choccie biscuits or elderflower juice (my fave) or something.

All my mates are kind. They invite me to sleep over at their houses when I lay the builder nightmare scenario on really thick – like last week I said that a plumber had caused a burst pipe and there was water everywhere. I like going to Georgie's place the best. It's awesome. They have five bedrooms at her house for just her and her mum. Five. And seeing as Georgie is an only child, that means they have three spare. Three. I wish I could go and live with her sometimes although I know deep down that I'd miss my family and especially the cats. Her house is like a palace compared to where I live, I feel like a princess when I'm there and her parents never interfere with her life. Not like my home. No privacy there. Not even in the bathroom as there was always someone knocking on the door telling whoever was in there to hurry up.

Some days, like today, being poor sucked. It was Friday. The twelfth of May. The whole world would be out enjoying the early summer sun this evening. Certainly half of our school would be. All down the local cinema complex to watch a movie and hang out. Some of the older girls from our school would also

187

be there, showing off fab new outfits they've just got. There would probably even be some boys there from Marborough High down the road. And I'll have to miss out on the whole outing because I haven't got enough money to go.

As we got up to go back into school, there was a sudden blast of wind blowing up dust and debris from the playground.

"Woah," said Georgie as her skirt billowed up. "Where's that come from?"

"Dunno," said Meg, "but let's run."

In an instant, more papers and toffee wrappers began to blow in a mini tornado around the playground as pupils headed back inside. A piece of paper flew towards me and stuck to my hand. I flicked it off but it fluttered back again and we all laughed because after I brushed it off for the second time, it seemed to follow me as we headed for the door back into the classrooms. It was dancing along behind me and just before I reached the door, it blew right up until it covered my face so that I couldn't see.

"Bleurgh," I blustered as I pulled it away from my eyes.

"Maybe it's meant for you," said Megan taking the paper away from me. "Let's see what it is."

"Yeah right," I said. "Maybe it's a message from a fairy." I was teasing her because last year, she was into fairies and angels and her bedroom was covered with posters of them.

"What does it say?" asked Hannah.

Megan scanned the paper. "Dear Tori, you are to go to the bluebell dell at midnight on Friday night…"

I punched her arm playfully. I knew she was making that up. "What does it really say?"

"It looks like some sort of promotion type thing," she replied. "Er… advertising local businesses kind of thing. A beauty salon in Osbury. A café/deli. An astrology site. Stuff like that."

"I'll chuck it," I said and took it to put in the outside litter bin in the corner of the playground. As I threw it away, there was a flash of lightening then a rumble of thunder in the distance. I glanced up. The sky had darkened threatening sudden rain so I raced back to join the others at the door.

"The fairies are angry that you threw away their business promotion," joked Georgie.

"Yeah right. Fairies and elves are alive and well and have taken over Osbury," I laughed back.

Seconds later, the skies opened and rain pelted down so we darted inside as quick as we could.

"Phew," I said as we raced along the corridors. "Just made it."

As we settled into class, our teacher Miss Wilkins was busy closing the windows that had been open earlier in the morning. The rain continued pouring down and the wind was still whipping up debris outside. As she reached the last window at the back of the class near my desk, a piece of paper blew in the window. It sailed right across the classroom and landed plonk in front of me.

Meg, Hannah and Georgie turned to look. I glanced down. It was the same piece of paper that had been following me in the playground! Beauty salon, deli, astrology website...

Maybe Megan was right and there were fairies and guardian angels out there. Maybe this was a message from one of them in code or something. *Yeah. And I'm the richest girl in the world,* I thought. However, the paper arriving in front of me did make me wonder. I didn't believe in fairyland like Meg but I *did* believe that some things are meant to be. Like fate. Or destiny. And this *was* a coincidence. I couldn't deny that. Maybe it *was* meant for me. I was about to put the paper in my rucksack to look at more carefully later when Miss Wilkins closed the last window and turned back to the class. As she did, she saw the paper that had landed on my desk.

"That rubbish is blowing everywhere!" she said as she picked it up, ripped it into tiny pieces and took it to the front where she put it into the bin. "Such a nuisance."

Oh no, I thought as I watched her do it. *There goes the message about my destiny – straight into the bin!*